Falling in love

Eliza Wood

Contents

Chapter 1

DAMMIT!WHAT THE FVCK IS WRONG WITH YOU ALL?

I WANT THIS PROJECT DONE BY TOMORROW! GOT IT?

"yes sir" All the employees said together, afraid of the man's words !

I cursed for the last time leaving for my cabin

I slammed the door open, walking inside my cabin.

I started working on my laptop typing aggressively.

That's when the door openedNobody dares to come inside my cabin without my permission.

"WHO THE FVCK-"

"Woahhhh woah calm down calm down bro" there comes my idiotic best friend AADVIK KAPOOR along with my another best friend LAKSHAY CHAUHAN

"The Fvck are you both doing here?" I asked frustratedly, I don't like it when someone invades my personal space, even if it's my best friends.

"We were gone just for a week and you changed so much " Aadvik exclaimed dramatically. Him and his dramatic ass.

"And what about this marriage shit ? got to know about your sudden marriage thingy so had to come running here" i heard lakshay express, well yeah i am getting married, to be honest I have literally no in interest in this. I am freaking forced to do this marriage.

I rolled my eyes at them, they are just too dramatic.

"It's nothing, and moreover I am not interested in this marriage, dadu forced me into this shit, knowing very well i won't deny him" i told them they looked at me in disbelief.

"Bro it's a High time now get over her" lakshay said keeping his hand over my shoulder.

"I told you thousands of times not to bring that topic-" i was cut off by Aadvik.

"Then Mr. Rajvansh when are you going to bring "that topic" of yours? huh? After an eternity or what?" Aadvik said sarcastically making me glare at him.

"For the first time I am agreeing with this idiot aadvik " lakshay said making Aadvik shoot a glare towards him.

"Guys i already told you , I AM OVER HER" i told them the matter of the fact.

"You are not lying to us abhi ! You are lying to yourself " said Aadvik.

"And yeah , abhi you can tell all this lies to everyone else, and they might believe it too, but we can see clearly through your lies" lakshay said joining in, i looked at them in a state of disbelief.

"I am leaving " i said walking out of my cabin . I know it that I am over her. But these idiots are not convinced yet. They think that I am still not over her.

I sighed.

Getting inside my car I drove off to the palace.

After 20 mins~

I am back at home and all the lights are off, maybe cause it's already midnight and everyone must be already sleeping.

Not thinking much I went to my room and dozed off.

~~~~~~~~~Prisha's POV

"Pri come on get up. You are going to be late for your classes." Someone calls out to me but I am still sleepy so I lay down lazily.

"Pri uth jaa. Aur kitna soyegi meri bacchi?" This time it was my baba who starts to shake me gently.

After a few more calls from my cutie baba i sat up straight.

"That's my good girl. Now, get ready for your college. Pehle hi bohot late hogaya hai, phir is chakkar mein tu breakfast nahi karti hai. Go take a bath." Baba says while kissing my forehead. I nod my head before getting inside the bathroom for my morning routine.

After getting dressed in a green kurti and a pair of black jeans I took my bag before going downstairs. I took blessings from my baba and maa. Baba kissed my forehead lovingly while maa just blankly nodded at me. I felt sad.

I went towards bhaiya and hugged him muttering a small "hare Krishna"

"God bless you baccha " he says while lovingly patting my head.
~~~~~~~~~

"You cheaters!!! Having all these sweet-sweet talks without me huh? Tum logo ne toh mujhe shadi se pehle hi paraya kar diya" I heard sneha di saying dramatically. Yeah you heard it right. She's getting married.

I giggled at my sweetheart that is my di. I Engulfed her in a hug.

"How can we forget you di?" I said, Looking at her lovingly, i genuinely adore her.

"Yes and if you dared to do so, then I'll tell you!" sneha di said in a joking manner.

After our lil talking session, we had our breakfast in silence and we all left for our respective works.

I usually go with Abhishek to my college, completing my breakfast I ran out of the house.

"Are pagal jaldi kar. Hum college ke liye late ho jayenge." Abhishek said as i hopped onto his bike and he drove off.

———————

After 15 mins we reached the college and ran to our classroom.

To our luck the teacher still hasn't arrived yet.

When the teacher came, all the students stood up in order to greet her. She started the class. When the bell rings indicating that the class has completed the teacher motions us to not leave the classroom, yet.

"Students I would like to inform you that the upcoming week our college will be hosting a Fresher's program for all the new students of the college. And as you are our freshers i wanted to let you'all know that, There will be your seniors too we want you all to cooperate with us. And not to forget to behave. Any sort of miss behaviour won't be tolerated. That's all for today. Now, you all can go now." The teacher says before getting out of the classroom I and Abhi got out of there.

"Ohhhhhhhh i seee someone is blushy-blushy huh?" Abhishek teased me.

"Stop it abhi" i said hiding my red cheeks, he's teasing me cause my crush is in the same college as me, i have had a crush on him since my highschool days. And he's going to come to the freshers party too, As he is our senior. Lemme tell you a lil secret. Just to get into the same college as him, I've worked my A$$ off. And here I am in the same college as him. Abhishek giggled and we again left for our classes....

That is how the day went.My college hours ended now i have to go back home! Huff! Well everyone loves me there but maa always reminds me that I am nothing but a burden to them.... Not by words though, but action speaks louder than words.... I never had a "home"I just had a house... But I am lucky to have baba, bhaiya, and di in my life

"Kaha khoyi hai? Ghar nahi chalna? Abhishek asked shaking my shoulder a bit.

"Kuch nahi, chal bohot der ho gayi hai mujhe Ghar chod de" i said.

He nodded

I hopped on to his bike and he dropped me back home.

As usual I had a smile on my faceLater we had dinner and everybody went to their respective rooms I too was very tired, so i decided to sleep early today....~~~~~~~

Chapter 2 : Nightmares

S o here's the new chapter Hope you enjoy itOhk then happy reading my Goofballs ____________◇◇◇______________Kya kahoon aankon ne meri sab keh diyaEk tuhi jene ka matalab keh diya Ab saansein chale na chele kya fikarTu chale saath toh khoobsurat safar Teri raahon mein Mera jaahan Ke rang lageya ishq da~Ke rang lageya ishq da~____________◇◇◇______________PRISHA'S POV

I started screening for help..."Nooo!! Please nooo !! Don't do this , i beg you please don't "

I felt someone shaking me trying to wake me up.

After several tries i finally opened my eyes and saw bhaiya and di beside me.. bhaiya engulfed me in a tight hug..

"Bacche, stop crying, it's ok! I am here na" bhaiya consoled me. While tears spilled out of my eyes, what was my fault? I thought.

"Pri kiddo please Rona band karo!! Shh it's fine!!" Di tried comforting me, nothing was fine, these panic attacks, this anxiety and the most horrible and terrible part about it......my Nightmares

I clung more onto bhaiya and cried a little more, feeling scared... While he just patted my back.

And before I knew i dozed off onto his shoulder.

Next morning~

I woke up from the annoying sound of my alarm, i looked beside me only to find di sleeping next to me holding my hand.. it's hard to believe that she is gonna get married soon . my di is gonna get married. I don't why but I feel like she's not happy with this marriage . Or maybe I am just overthinking it!I sighed, shrugging off my thoughts i planted a soft and loving kiss on her forehead.

I got freshened and wore a pretty navy blue coloured saree pairing it up with jhumka and my precious anklet.

Di too was with her morning routine, we both decided to step downstairs for breakfast!!!

"Good morning everyone" i said as soon as I entered the dining room.

"Good morning baccha" baba and bhaiya said at the exact same time.

While maa just blankly nodded, i passed her a small smile.We all dined in, as we all were busy devouring our breakfast, that's when Maa said..

"They're going to come tomorrow " maa said breaking the silence.. by "they" maa meant the "RAJVANSH FAMILY"

Di's spoon fell off her hands, i faced her, i can see how pale di looks right now. Is she ok? I thought. The chain of my thoughts broke when Maa exclaimed "And i don't want prisha in that moment in this house" maa said breaking the leftover pieces of my heart...

"But- " baba tried to say something but I cut him off in the middle .

"baba it's ok, I can stay at Abhi's place and moreover it's not a big deal." I tried convincing them.

"Baccha-" bhaiya was cut off in between, i knew he would try to convince me to stay here only, but I can't afford to ruin Maa's mood.

"It's ok Bhai" i said masking my face with a beautiful smile.

"Ok so I am leaving for the college" i said and walked out before planting a kiss over Baba's cheeks.

"Take care pri" i heard bhaiya say before i disappeared out of the house.

"I will " i said running out of the house.

OUTSIDE THE HOUSE ~

"heyyyy" Abhi greeted me as soon as he noticed me.

"happy birthday to you~Nobody likes you, you look like an animal, go back to the zoo~i said singing him a birthday song and engulfing him in a hug." I sang this lil birthday song for him, after all he's the birthday boy today!!

"Hehe thanks priii !! Where's my gift?" He asked, and I pulled out a bracelet and made him wear it.

"Awww thank youuuuuu " he exclaimed while i just dramatically bowed at him.

"You okay " Abhi asked me as soon as he noticed "my famous fake Smile "

"I am " i said as I tried hiding my gloomy face from him.

"Pri don't lie" he spoke thinning his eyebrows.

And i felt a lone tear slipping out of my eye."Abhi can I stay at your apartment for tomorrow?" I finally asked him.

"Pagal ye bhi koi puchne ki baat hai? Jo Mera hai vo Tera hai. Or Jo Tera hai vo Mera hai , bhul gayi kya?" He exclaimed wiping off my tears.

"Btw , i see someone is looking beautiful today" Abishek spoke in a teasing manner."what's with this makeup-shakeup huh? Trying to impress someone or what?"

"Stop it na Abhi" i whined and he laughed at my frustrated face.

"Ok let's go then?" He asked offering me his hand.

I giggled and held his hand and we left for our college.

Abhi and I have been friends since our childhood ! He's the child of my parents best friend.. so basically we are beside each other since our diaper days. Hehe. That is why he's so close to me. He can see through the lies that I go around telling people..

He's basically like a brother to me... I am lucky to have him in my life. I cannot thank God enough for this idiotic brother of mine.

We reached the college~

"Chale?" I asked him, holding his hand in a firm yet a gentle way.

"Haan chal" he said and we both walked out hand in hand in the college. He knows very well that i have social anxiety that's why he always helps me reduce it by grabbing my hands while going into any sort of a crowded place.

After the classes we started leaving for the event but before that we grabbed a small cake, and decorated it with candlesticks , and celebrated his birthday.

At the event ~

The party was at its peak Right now maybe cause of how late we are... It's already 5. 30.

Everybody was dancing and enjoying themselves.

I too participated in one of these compititions, tbh I was forced to. Of course Abhishek did.

Just then we heard an announcement, it was from our senior and also our CR of the music department.

"Thank you all for joining us enlightening this event . Now i would like to invite miss prisha " He stated.

"Priiiii please gooo it's your time to shine, dekh bhagwan bhi yahi chahata hai go ahead and show everyone what you are capable of" he encouraged me.

"I sure I'll mess up, what if I ended up making a mess there?" i exclaimed while shaking my head.

"Please pri ! Tu hamesha Mera nahi sunti, tu agar nahi jaayegi na toh mein rudra ko bata dunga ki tujhe uspar crush hai" he told me smirking, Aghhhhhh he's a born blackmaler.

"Ohkkk fine" i said before getting up.

I went to the stage and held the mic in my shivering hands before i closed my eyes, taking a deep breath in and I started singing..

The one that I am singing is one of my favourites , it is because i have witnessed my parents perform on this soothing song several times. They were my favourite couple to ever exist.

Lag Ja Gale Ki Phir Ye Hasin Raat Ho Na Ho

Shaayad Phir Is Janam Men Mulaaqaat Ho Na Ho

Lag Jaa Gale ...

Ham Ko Mili Hain Aaj, Ye Ghadiyaan Nasib Se

Ji Bhar Ke Dekh Lijiye Ham Ko Karib SePhir Aap Ke Nasib Men Ye Baat Ho Na HoShaayad Phir Is Janam Men Mulaaqaat Ho Na Ho

Lag Jaa Gale ...

Paas Aaiye Ki Ham Nahin Aaenge Baar-Baar.

Baahen Gale Men Daal Ke Ham Ro Le Zaar-Zaar.

Aankhon Se Phir Ye Pyaar Ki Barasaat Ho Na Ho.

Shaayad Phir Is Janam Men Mulaaqaat Ho Na Ho.

Lag Ja Gale Ki Phir Ye Hassin Raat Ho Na Ho.

Shaayad Phir Is Janam Men Mulaaqaat Ho Na Ho.

Lag Jaa Gale...

As i completed the last note of it I heard the sound of Everybody clapping for me. My parents would have been so proud of me.

I stepped down the stage. Only to be engulfed in a bone crashing hug.

" I am really proud of you my gurl. You sang so perfectly. Now my bestie is a star. YAYYYYYY. I love you priiiii" He said dramatically while hugging me tightly.

We walked out, talking about random stuff.

I noticed Abhi's eyes getting bigger as he stared behind me. Being confused turned around to see who the person was. However, by seeing the person in front of me my words died down deep in my throat.

"Sorry to bother you but I come here to let you know that you have sung very well today and you have great vocals And also not to forget you look very pretty today" I BLUSHED. And the person was none other than.............

RUDRA RANAWAT

MY CRUSH!

Ahh-th-ank-s i shuttered clearly fluttered by hearing him complimenting me.

He smirked probably from the effect he has on me.

"Ohk so guys I am leaving now, Take care prisha" he says before leaving.

"HOLY FVCK WHAT JUST HAPPENED HERE? IS IT REAL? OH GOD SOMEONE PINCH ME PLEASE-" I cut him off in middle.

"Shhh...shut up abhi stop being dramatic" i say shhshing him while hiding my red burning cheeks.

"It was my birthday but it seems like you got the gift instead" he said while my cheeks heat up.

"Blushy-blushy huh?" He teased me making me more red.

"Stop ittttttttttttttttttttttttt " he laughed at my antics.

"Abhi sun? Ghar chale? " I ask getting normal again.

"As you wish Mrs. ranawat" saying this he ran away, while i chased him.~
~~~~~~~~~~~~~~~~~~~

This is it for todaySo the 2nd chapter is hereeeeeeeee What do you think? What could be the reason of her nightmaresDon't worry I'm gonna reveal it in upcoming chapters.Lemme know how it was?Don't forget to
~~~~~~~~~~~~~~~~~~~

vote!!!!!Vote target 40 !!I'll upload the next chapter once the target is done

Byeeeeeeee my Goofballs~~~~~~~~~~~~~~

Chapter 3: The first sight

So here's the new chapter Hope you enjoy itOhk then happy reading my Goofballs □__________✧✧✧_____________Dekha hazaron dafa aapkoPhir bekarari kaise haiSambhale sambhalta nahi ye dilKuch aapme baat esi hai_________✧✧✧_____________ABHIMAN'S POV

"Abhiman where were you last night" dad asked me as soon as i entered the dining room.

"Office" i replied in my monotonous voice Making Maa sigh.

"We are going to Delhi tomorrow and for that we are going to leave today." Dad disclosed the news.

"Ohk" that's all I uttered cause it's of no use to argue with him.

"I have to attend a program in Delhi, today so I am leaving for it... Text me the address I'll be there Tomorrow" i said getting up from the dining table.

Hearing upon me , He just nodded his head.

AT DELHI AIRPORT ~

I am currently in the Delhi airport waiting for the car that is going to pick me up. ....

The driver came and he greeted me, I simply nod my head before getting inside the car. I am here only for the college program and to meet the family of my soon to be wife. I reached the reception desk to fetch the keys for the room I have booked earlier. Getting the keys i made my way towards my room.. after getting freshened up i decided to leave for the event.

At the college~

(What he's wearing-)

I reached the location where I was informed.

"I think we should get going towards the auditorium. It's time to start the program." Principal Sir says in which I nod my head in answer.

We talked about the college on our way.

The teachers and the students greeted me, to which I just replied in a very cold tone, later I was requested to come on the stage.

Reaching upon there i took the microphone in my hand everybody starts to cheer loudly for me which made me smile a little seeing the excitement they had to hear me.

"Thank you so much for inviting me here. i will just say that focus on what you want and what you want to achieve. In the end it's always going to be you who is going to make you achieve the things that you want." All the students start to clap.

After a few minutes of speech, I came back from the stage before taking a seat beside the Principal. There were several performances made after that. there come a boy, maybe about to announce Something.

"Thank you all for joining us and enlightening this event with your presence, now i would like to invite miss prisha on stage" He statedAnd after a min I saw a girl standing up and walking towards the stage…. Andddddddd i swear she's the prettiest girl I've ever seen. And the fact I am not even embarrassed of admitting this.

I was so lost in my thoughts, that's when the chain of my thoughts broke when i heard a soothing voice..

The song that she's singing right now is one of my favourites.

Lag Ja Gale Ki Phir Ye Hasin Raat Ho Na HoShaayad Phir Is Janam Men Mulaaqaat Ho Na HoLag Jaa Gale …Ham Ko Mili Hain Aaj, Ye Ghadiyaan Nasib SeJi Bhar Ke Dekh Lijiye Ham Ko Karib SePhir Aap Ke Nasib Men Ye Baat Ho Na HoShaayad Phir Is Janam Men Mulaaqaat Ho Na HoLag Jaa Gale …Paas Aaiye Ki Ham Nahin Aaenge Baar-BaarBaahen Gale Men Daal Ke Ham Ro Le Zaar-ZaarAankhon Se Phir Ye Pyaar Ki Barasaat Ho Na HoShaayad Phir Is Janam Men Mulaaqaat Ho Na HoLag Ja Gale Ki Phir Ye Hassin Raat Ho Na HoShaayad Phir Is Janam Men Mulaaqaat Ho Na HoLag Jaa Gale…

Everybody clapped for her as she gracefully steeped down the stage and walked towards a guy and hugged him TIGHTLY- i widened my eyes. who is he ? Why did she hug him-What the hell! am i jealous? No, ain't no way! I am going to get married soon and What the actual Fvck am i even thinking?

I have to leave this place as soon as possible. I am really tired, i should get some sleep..the work is actually taking over me. I must be out of my mind thinking this way. *It isn't the work, it's that girl taking over your mind** my subconscious mind interrupted. What is happening to me? It's not even a proper hour i have seen this girl and she's already all over my mind. Abhiman you need to rest. I've to go to my would be wife's house too..

After an hour I left the event and went to the room that I booked, to get some sleep...

Tomorrow I have to meet her family...What's her name again? Shrisha ? No. Shruti? Nahh. YEAHHHH her name is Sneha. Sneha singhania Let's see what's gonna happen tomorrow.

~~~~~~~~~~~~~~This is it for todayNew chapter is hereeeeeeeee Goofballs Lemme know how it was?Don't forget to vote!!!!!Vote target 40 !!I'll upload the next chapter once the target is done Byeeeeeeee my Goofballs

.
~~~~~~~~~~~~~~

Chapter 4: fixing the dates

So here's the new chapter Hope you enjoy itOhk then happy reading my Goofballs ___________◇◇◇_______________Teri Nazar mein , nayi si ada hai Naya sa nasha bhi, ghula hai~___________◇◇◇_______________ABHIMAN'S POVI woke up and did my morning routine before walking out of the hotel I wore a black tuxedo pairing up with black shoes

I saw the text message from dad.

The address was pretty far from here it will probably take me 2 hours to get there.

While I was thinking about it. my driver from yesterday appeared infront of me.. he bowed at me I just nodded my head before getting into the car.

I drove off.

I was scrolling through Instagram just then a message popped up on my screen, it was from aadvik and lakshay. We had a separate group on Instagram.

ON THE PHONE~

The rich people

The_sassy_kapoor : best of luck bro

The_lakshay: same here dude

Abhiman_singh_rajvansh: Fvck off

And that's how I closed my insta..

I started checking and reading my files until i arrived at singhania mension. Ofcourse what else should I do? Waste my precious time over this marriage, that I am not even interested in?

The driver dropped me out.

I fixed my tux before ringing the bell cause my family has already arrived.

A maid opened the door for me and led me where others were present.

The singhania's got up and bowed at me in respect.

I greeted them and they too greeted me back.

I got settled beside Yash. He passed me a cheeky smile and as usual i rolled my eyes at him.

Both the families started talking and I was the least interested in all the talks happening around. I just answered when somebody asked me something.

Just then I heard a ring that sounded similar to that of the phone's.

I looked up only to find, It was rishab's.

"Excuse me it's an important call" he says before walking out of the room.

Being unbothered my eyes unintentionally fell on my soon to be wife.

She was looking lost. And unbothered just like me, i could tell that she doesn't want this marriage. Then why isn't she saying anything?

As I was thinking about this stuff Rishabh came back while stuffing his phone back in his pocket.

"Who was it beta?" Maa asked rishab, Rishabh looked at Maa before answering.

"My sister" rishab says, making my mother nod.

"Bhaisahab aapki do betiya hai?" I heard dad asking uncle. Well he has another daughter? As if i care.

"Jii, she's in college right now" uncle replied back to my father.

"Acha" maa said with a small smile appearing on her face.

"What's her name?" Chachi asked, there She goes again I know what she is trying to do right now, I took a look over dharya.

"Prisha" sneha says opening her mouth for the first time in this whole time.

"How old is she?" I heard my Chachi asking. I heard dharya sigh.

"She's 21" rishab says.

"She'll be perfect for my dharya , I'll love to meet her someday" Chachi said, as I already knew this was why she was asking for her name and age.

"Ofcourse" uncle says, as uncle said this a huge smile crept over chachi's face.

"So Bhaisahab I've asked our pandit ji and he gave us 3 dates one is after two weeks and then second one is after an year. We want this marriage as soon as possible... If you agree we'll start the preparations then?" maa asked them politely not trying to force her decisions on the Singhania family.

"Isn't it too early bhenji?" Uncle said, he looked tensed.

"Mujhe pata hai but don't worry we will manage everything " maa immediately replied back as she understood why uncle was tensed, maybe because of how everything will be arranged in such a short span of time.

"So i guess everything is done now we should take our leave" dadu said and dadi nodded. The Singhania family look at each other's faces and nodded.

"Ohk then we'll start the preparations " aunty exclaimed.

Everybody starts to leave and at last i got up.

"Ohk uncle then I'll take my leave "i said in a monotonous way.

"Beta abb hum ek pariwar ka hissa banne Jaa rahe hai don't call me uncle call me baba " uncle-i mean baba told me.

"Ohk baba" i said as I bent down to touch his feets, he kept his palm over my head, and blessed me. I bid my goodbye and left their house.

We got inside our cars and left for the airport.

~~~~~~~~Prisha's POV

I woke up early todayI did my usual morning routine. After getting done with it i wore my chickenkari kurti pairing it up with jutti (a type of foot wear)

(What she's wearing)

and quickly rushed over to wake di up.

"Wake up didiiiiiiiiiiiiiiiiiiiiiiiiiiiiiiiiiiiiiiiiiiiiiiiiiii" i called out for her while gently shaking her.

She got up and hugged me all of a sudden...
~~~~~~~~

"You okayyy di?" I asked being confused, She didn't say anything just hugged me tighter. Making me worried for her.

I too didn't say anything and hugged her back. I gently patted her back in order to comfort her.

After sometime, She pulled back from the hug.

"I am okay" she replied back to me although I was not convinced but I decided to let it go.

"So today someone is going to see someone huh?" I teased her, in a manner to distract her from whatever that was troubling her.

"Yeah..." She didn't blush or had that shy expression that girls usually do, while talking about their future husbands.. rudra is just my crush but i myself blush when someone mentions Rudra's name.

"You're happy with this marriage right di?" I asked her while she just nodded her head i could feel that something's off about this marriage shit or maybe i am just overthinking it.?

"Ohk then take care of yourself i am leaving for my college now Abhi must be waiting for me" i said, deciding to let it go and convincing myself that it was just all my over thinking and nothing was wrong with this marriage.

"Pri can't you just stay at home? I promise I'll convince maa " di said more like pleaded.

I sighed, i know my presence will only ruin maa's mood. And I cannot afford to ruin anybody's mood.

"Di, i just want to keep maa happy if she's happy without me then let it be.. and it's not a big deal.. and yeah if you are nervous then just take a deep breath and everything will be fine. I am sure jiju will be smitten , looking at this beauty of yours" i said giggling I thought that she would blush or something but she did not. I can't help myself but overthink it.

"Ohk then take care of yourself baccha" di said and i nodded before heading out of the room

I walked out of the house and saw Abhi wait for me.

"Heyyyyyyy" he said as he noticed me.

"Hiii " i replied.

"Chale? He asked.

"Chal " i said hopping onto his bikeAnd he drove off.

We reached the college and went to attend our classes.

AFTER THE CLASSES ~

All the student must have gone by now but both I and Abhishek are still in the library as of because we have to complete our pending assignments and also to study for the upcoming exams.

"huff!! Let's go i am so tired " Abhi said as he was finally done with his pending assignments.

"Let's go then " i replied, I too was done with my studies and I also completed my assignment.

"PRISHA " someone yelled my name. I turned around to look who yelled out my name only to find Rudra walking towards us.

I widened my eyes and looked at Abhi who just smirked at me. Please don't tell me that Abhishek is going to leave me with him alone.

"Hi" rudra greeted me with a pleasant smile over his face.

"Hey" i replied lowering my gaze. At this moment I just wanted to hide myself because of how shy I am feeling right now.

"Ohk so I'll be at the entrance of our college pri come after talking to sir " he said winking at me before leaving me with rudra. This idiot!!!!!! I'll see him after this.

"Sir you had some work?" I asked in a very respectful manner because he is my senior and I should show respect towards him.

"First of all call me rudra. And second of all can't I talk to you normally? I don't have any work for you, don't worry " he said making my cheeks heat up, i looked up at him, lifting my gaze.

I widened my eyes as I saw the scene unfolding in front of my eyes.

HE FREAKING KNELT DOWN ON HIS HOLLY KNEES AND THEN HE PULLED OUT A FREAKING ROSE ARGHHHH-HHHH. My eyes must be looking as big as a socket.

"So i want to say that I love you. I love you very much, From the moment I've seen you. I didn't believe in love at all, but it was before you walked into my life. I have loved you when I saw you at the school for the first time with those dangling ponytails. You are in my mind 24/7. And I cannot tend to take you out of my mind it's just too impossible for me. Will you be my girlfriend pri? Are you willing to be mine forever? He said making my eyes tear up. This was the day I waited the most.

"Heyy why are you crying? I am sorry if I made you uncomfortable " he asked immediately getting up and cupping my cheeks.

And I did what my heart told me to. I hugged him.

"YESS" i replied to his confession he made, and sobbed hiding my face in his chest.

"Don't cry love! Please stop crying it breaks my heart" rudra said while rubbing my back in a soothing manner.

"I love you too rudra, i have loved you from the moment I've seen you. I just didn't have the courage to confess it . thank youuuuuu for being my first love and thank you for choosing me."I said between my sobs.

"Baba stop crying naa" he said, caressing my back.

I pulled back from the hugAnd looked at him shyly. I swear I must be looking like a red tomato.

"Aww you look so cute while blushing" he said kissing my cheeks.

I widened my eyes and he chuckled seeing my expressions.

"Get used to it jaan, I'll be doing a lot more just than kissing your cheeks" he says making my cheeks more red.

"I'll b-e going the-n Abhi m-ust be wait-ing fo-r me" i said pulling apart from the hug, I cannot take it anymore I am just too shy, I uttered out, hurriedly walking towards the entrance.

"BYE GIRLFRIEND" i heard him yellingI just Chuckled going towards Abhi.

"What was it? What did he said? What did he talked about so long? AND WAIT A MINUTE WHY DO YOU HAVE A FVCKING ROSE IN YOUR HOLY HANDS ? WHY IS YOUR FACE COVERED WITH TEARS?- he said as soon as he noticed me. What should I even do with this man?

"Take a deep breath " he did as i instructed him"Now tell me what happened?" He inquired.

" woh-me-in I- woh-" i shuttered, I was not able to say what happened a while ago.

"Tell me clearly pri i can't understand what you are trying to say" he asked impatiently.

"He-he proposed me " i said shutting my eyes tightly, as I knew what was coming next..

"WHAT THE ACTUAL FVCK?" he said, completely shocked.

"Yeah" i say, meanwhile my cheeks heat up.

"YAYYYYYY finally your one-sided love story comes to an end. i am so happy pri. Finally you'll know what those bookish kinda love feels like. I am so happy that there will be someone else other than me who'll take care of you. Congratulations bestie " he said getting happy for me and hugged me tightly.

"Thankyou Abhi" i said hugging him back.

"Let's celebrate " he said out of a sudden.

"Ohk then the Bill's up to me " i said making him smile widely.

"But first let me inform bhaiya that I am going to stay with you tonight " i told him dialing bhaiya's number.

OTP ~

He picked it up

"Hi Bhai" i greeted him in a cheerful voice.

"Hi bacha everything okay?" Bhai asked me over the phone.

"Haan bhaiya everything is fine you tell me how's everything going there" i replied and questioned back.

"Well until now everything is going smoothly " bhaiya replied back calmly.

"Umm bhaiya I'll be staying at Abhi's place tonight is that ok?" I asked praying to God for him to give me the permit .

"You don't need my permission sweetheart you can go anywhere you want just take care of yourself okay?" He said sweetly while my heart swelled up with respect and love for my Bhai.

"Ohk Bhai" i replied back to him, with a small smile glistening over my lips.

"Ohk then bye kiddo take care of yourself" Bhai said before i hung up

"You too bhaiya " and I hung up the call. I turned back to face Abhi.

"Let's go Abhi" i exclaimed and i nodded.

"Chal" he said and he drove off to his apartment.

We danced , sang songs, watched movies, and at last getting tired we slept on the couch itself.

~~~~~~~~~~~~That's it for today Hope you enjoyed the chapterI'll be posting the chapters again as soon as i am done with my examinations. Until then bye and take care my Goofballs □Don't forget to vote, maybe I'll post something, Hehe
~~~~~~~~~~~~

Chapter 5: shopping

P risha's POV

I woke up rubbing my eyes and I felt some weight over my lap only to find Abhi sleeping keeping his head on my lap. I Chuckled remembering our childhood. He's like this since our childhood.

I decided not to disturb him as it's Sunday today.

I went to the washroom and got freshened up. I have come here many times so I knew the directions already. Uncle and aunty lives in their hometown. Gujarat. They used to live here but a year back they decided to move their business to Gujarat.

Getting freshened up i made my way towards Abhi, it's already 11: 30 in the morning.

"Abhiii ! uth ja mereko Ghar chod de bohot late ho gaya hai" i said waking him up. But him being a Goblin he did not even move a inch.

"Sone de na yarrrrrrrrrrr " he said.stubbornly not wanting to wake up.

"Please naa Maa bohot dategi mujhe" i said pleading him.

"Rudra ko bol de, waise bhi ab vo Tera boyfriend hai. Or vo subha uth bhi gya hoga, gym vim mein hoga" he said covering himself with the blanket. I whined frustratedly.

"Yarrrrrrrrrrr uth na" i said to which he didn't replied anything.

"Tujhe dekhkar toh kumbhkaran bhi sharma jai" i said picking up my phone and dialing Rudra's number

"You can do it pri ! Go ahead!" I mumbled to myself. I nervously dialled his number.

After 2 rings he picked up the call..

"Heyy" he greeted me as soon as he got on line.

"Hi" i replied nervously.

"Rudra i need a help" i hesitated-ly spoke.

"Hukum kariye or Banda hazir hoga " he replied back vanishing all my nervousness.

"Umm can you pick me up from Abhishek's house?" I asked hoping he would not deny me.

"As in your best friend Abhishek?" He asked back.

"Yeah"

"Text me the address I'll be there " he spoke making me smile.

"Thank you Rudra " i thanked him. Only to receive flirty reply in return.

"You're welcome girlfriend " he said in a teasing manner.

I hung up the call being a blushing mess.

I texted him the address.

After 10 mins ~

I heard a horn outside I went to the balcony and I saw a car standing just outside the apartment.

I guess rudra is here. I thought to myself before heading towards Abhishek to inform him that I was going.

"Abhi i am going, take care of yourself and don't forget to have your breakfast " i strictly told him as I was well aware of his nature of skipping meals.

"Ohk tu Jaa or jab pohunch jaaegi tab text kar Dena " he mumbled sleepily. This man and his obsession with sleeping.

"Byee kumbhkaran" i Said rushing out of the house.

I saw rudra waiting for me inside his car.

"Hii" he said opening up the cars door for me as he noticed my presence.

"Heyy" i replied back with a shy smile. Why do I feel so shy around him?

"Get in" he exclaimed and I nodded before getting inside the car.

"Thank you for coming on such short notice" i said being grateful of him.

"Arey koi na, ab toh ye sab chalta hi rahega " he said smiling towards me and i reciprocated.

"You look beautiful by the way" he said.

"I am literally in yesterday's outfit" i giggled, did he not notice my dress yesterday?

"It doesn't matter what you wear you will always be beautiful for me" he said looking at me lovingly, I just blushed and we chatted all along the way.

After 15 mins~

I stepped out of the car as we reached my home.

"Ohk then thanks for the ride I'll meet you tomorrow at the college" i said smiling towards him

"Ohk then have a nice day ahead girlfriend" him and his nicknames that he gives me will be the death of me someday.

I watched his car disappear. And I left for my home.~~~~~~~~~~~~~~~I reached home and as soon as I stepped in i dropped a text to Abhi.

I climbed up to my room only to find di standing at the door.with a suspicious gaze?

"Where were you last night?" She inquired.

"At Abhi's place " i replied truthfully.

"Then who was the person who dropped you ?" She asked making me widen my eyes.

"It-it- wa-s a fri-end" i said nervously.

"Pri lying is a bad habit. You shouldn't lie when you don't know how to" she scolded me with a accusing stare.

"I-t was my bo-yfri-end" i said looking down. Now I was genuinely scared and I did not know how di is doing to react.

"OHH MY FUCKING GOD" she said FREAKING out.

"Dii shhh" i tried to calm her down. But was she in the mood of calming down? NO.

"When? How? Where? Why? I want to know all of it and dare you to lie" she said throwing questions at me she looked rather excited.

I told her about all the things from my Highschool to today's date.

"Oh my god all this was happening and you didn't tell me huh?" She said teasing me.

"Sorry di" i said holding my ears, I looked at her making puppy eyes knowing very well they will surely melt her.

" it's ok , but I see someone is having a boyfriend huh?" Now it was her teasing me, the tables are changed.

I Blushed, I am going to die because of how much I am blushing today everyone has set up a task to make me blush I guess.

"Leave me tell me about yourself what happened yesterday?" I asked turning the tables, and I can clearly see how her smile faded.

"Nothing happened they just fixed the date of my marriage and they want it as soon as possible and for that we won't be having any rituals we will just be getting married. And we are going for shopping today. And i dare you to deny coming with us." She said pointing a finger at me. What does she mean by they won't be having any rituals?

"So you mean you'll just get married without any rituals? No haldi? No mehendi? No sangeet? No engagement? I said widening my eyes.

"Yes." She sighed.

"How can they do that!!!?!! I planned so much for your wedding! Mere sare plan par Pani pher Diya" i huffed being annoyed. I so wanted to make this marriage special for my sister but look what is happening here!

"It's ok pri you go get ready we will be leaving in an hour for the shopping " di said and i nodded before heading towards the washroom.

I took a shower and wore my fav kurti.

I got ready and was about to head downstairs but then i received a call My phone displayed "RUDRA"I quickly received the call

"Hey future wifey " he said and i Blushed but i decided to play along this time.

"Hi future husband" i said still blushing, but not letting it affect my voice.

"So what's going on?" He asked casually in a very polite and sweet manner.

"Kuch nahi , di ki shadi final ho gayi hai toh shopping ke liye Jaa Rahi thi" i said and he hummed.

"So after your shopping, date par chale?" He asked making me shocked because I did not expect him to say this. Not so early. we just started dating yesterday only.

"Haan?" I asked confirming, thinking I might have heard something wrong.

" what "Haan " i asked do you wanna go to a date after your shopping is done?" He asked once again, he kinda sounded impatient.

"Yes" i slowly whispered shyly, it was just a mere whisper.

"Ohk then meet you at the date wifey " he said before hanging up.

I giggled to myself thinking about his words.

I went downstairs and all of us left for shopping.

~~~~~~~~~~~~~Abhiman's POV
~~~~~~~~~~~~~

"Can't you all just go alone dadu?" I asked my dadu who refused stubbornly.

"I said what i said you are coming with us and that's final i am not hearing a word against my decision " dadu said more like ordered me. And I cannot go against any decision made by my grandfather I respect him a lot.

" Abhi go and get ready " maa told me and I frustratedly nodded before answering her.

"Fine" i said being done with my family.

I got ready.

(Ignore the glass in his hand)

And i went downstairs and we all headed towards the mall.

Let's see what future awaits......~~~~~~~~~~~~Yeayyy so New chapter is hereeeeeeeeeeHope you liked it And yeah that's it for today

Chapter 6: first encounter

So here's the short update Hope you enjoy itOhk then happy reading my Goofballs __________✧✧✧__________Teri Aankhiyan ne kar dita pagal das ki karaRatan nu menu neend na aave tere bina Soni aaja mere kol tu aa Hun aake dur na javiHaye hogai pyar tere na __________✧✧✧__________

Abhiman's POV

We reached the mall and started waiting for the singhania s to appear.While waiting for them i received a call from my PA i excused myself and went outside to attend the call.

As I was done with the conversation I turned around and was about to head back to my family, and that's when a little figure bumped into me.

Whoever it was, was about to fall but I held her by her waist.

She had her eyes closed tightly while she clutched onto my collar tightly probably scared of falling down. WAIT- I've seen her before.

OHHH FVCKKKKKKKKKKKKKKKKKKKKK the college girl.

She opened her eyes ever so slowly. And that's when everything seemed to be stopped around me , I kept staring at those hazel brown eyes of hers.

I saw her blinking her eyes, making me Realise the position we were in. I removed my hands from her waist, even though I wished I could hold her more. Maybe a little more won't hurt, no?

"I am sorry for recklessly walking and colliding into you" she said with her angelic voice.

"It's ok" i said keeping my face neutral like it wasn't a big deal, knowing very well that if it was someone else he/she would be 6 feet down the ground. She smiled at me before leaving. I kept staring at her, walking away, until she disappeared.

Author's POV

Sorry for distributing you all but you must be wondering why Prisha didn't recognise Abhiman.

It's because she still doesn't know with whom her di is getting married to. She just knew that it was someone from the rajvansh family. Hope it's clear now. Continue reading.

Back to the story~

I was confused about why I decided to let her go, did I just forgive Some-one? I seriously need to drag myself to a good psychiatrist, i think I am loosing my mind. I sighed before walking towards my family.~~~~~~~~~ ~~~~~~Prisha's POV

We all reached the mallWe started walking where the Rajvansh family was.

"Oh shit " sneha di said making me halt.

"What happened di?" I asked in confusion.

"I forgot my phone in the car" she replied.

"I can get it for you. Go ahead I'll be there" i said with an assuring nod, and she nodded her head and headed inside.

I turned around walking towards the car to fetch Di's phone.

After getting it I made my way where everyone was.

On my way i bumped into something. I had my eyes tightly closed ,out of fear. I clutched something that i found, in order to not let myself fall. I felt two hands snaking my waist.

I opened my eyes ever so slowly. Just to get them locked with those choco-late brown eyes.

I kept staring at those chocolate brown orbs. I realized his hands were wrapped around me, i blinked my eyes, letting him realise the position we were in.

He took his hands off of me. I apologized for being a reckless fellow and bumping into him. All he said was "it's ok", i smiled at him before walking away.

Walking for a while , i found my di i went towards her.

"Here! Your phone " i said handing her, her phone.

"Meet my sister . PRISHA. Prisha singhania. " i heard bhaiya say as I turned around only to find a family staring at me.

My subconsciousness told me that they were the rajvansh.

"Khama ghani" i said bowing my head a little.

"Ghani khama" A lady said in a loving manner.

I just smiled sweetly towards her.

"So if everyone is here shall we proceed with the shopping?" A beautiful girl maybe in her early 20s said with excitement clear in her voice.

"Yess please?" A guy said who looked in his early 20s .

"Ohk then let go" Maa said, making everyone agree.

We all nodded just then another guy appeared in front of us.

"Sorry for being late" i widened my eyes seeing the person in front of me. It was the same man i bumped into earlier. He too widened his eyes before masking it with neutral expressions.

"Abhiman let's go na. Already bohot late ho gaya hai" that sweet aunty from earlier said."Ohk" that unknown man that i suppose is named Abhiman exclaimed.

"Di who are you getting married to? There are a total of 3 boys here" i whisper asked di.

"Abhiman. The guy who just came." She said and i nodded before heading behind her.~~~~~~~~~~~~~~~~~~~~Ahh I apologise for this short update but i swear I'll make up to you □Ohk so my goofballs don't forget to voteAnd yeah that's it for today ~~~~~~~~~~~~~~~~~~~~

Chapter 7: shopping pt.2

So here's this short update Hope you enjoy itOhk then happy reading my Goofballs ____________ ✧✧✧ _______________Tera mera rishta hai kaisaEk pal dur gavaara nahiTere liye har roz hai jeetetujhko Diya mera vakt sabhi____________ ✧✧✧ ________________

We walked inside the mall and started exploring the mall.

Di showed 0 interest in all this while, while shopping. I felt a sharp gaze at me . I turned around only to see those chocolate brown orbs staring straight into my soul.

I quickly turned around, as i sensed Something odd when he looked at me. That was when my phone rang, and " Rudra " displayed on the screen of my phone.

Di was standing just beside me, hearing the sound of my phone, she looked at me with a teasing stare while I just blushed.

"Go outside and answer it" she whispered to me while I shyly nodded before walking outside.

"Hello" I greeted.

"Hey future wifey! Done with the shopping?" He asked.

"Nahi, abhi toh start Kari hai" i replied.

"Yarrrrrrrrrr text me the address I want to see you I am coming there" i widened my eyes, hearing upon him.

"No rudra you can't come here" immediately exclaimed.

"WHYYYYYY" he said more like whined exactly like a kid.

"Because my family's here, and i can't afford to get caught by them" i said giggling while he whined.

"Please?????" He said in a kid's voice and i melted.

"Rudra will meet tomorrow na? Please?" I said trying to convince him.

"Fineeeeeeee" he gave in.

"Ohk then will talk to you later byeee hubby" i said giggling before hanging up the call.

Hanging up the call, i walked inside the mall.

"Prii come here see this it's so beautiful " di exclaimed.

"Coming " i said walking towards her.

"Wowwwwwwww" the words slipped off my mouth as soon as i saw the mangalsutra

(The mangalsutra)

"You should definitely buy this, it even matches the initial of jiju" i told her, upon which she shook her head.

"It's not my type " she spoke still shaking her head.

"But it's so beautiful " i said while pouting, trying to convince her.

"If it had the initial of rudra i would have definitely bought this" i thought.

"Leave it " she said as she walked away , she started exploring other stuff. but i still had my eyes on that mangalsutraI sighed before walking towards her.

"Everything done ladies?" I heard a husky voice say.~~~~~~~~~~~~~~~~~~~~~~~~~Abhiman's POV

All the girls went towards the ladies section while all the men went towards the men's section.

I was busy selecting my clothes before I received a call.

I went outside to attend the call, I was done with my call when I heard a soothing voice.

It was prisha's voice, she was on video call with someone, her being on a video call was the reason i could listen to their conversation very easily.

Hello?" She greeted."Hey future wifey! Done with the shopping?" I heard a manly voice exclaim, and i swear i could feel the anger bubbling inside me.

"Nahi, abhi toh start Kari hai" she replied to that idiotic creature.

"Yarrrrrrrrrrrr text me the address I want to see you I am coming there" that bivth told her,making my eyes bloodshot. First of all, why am I behaving like this? It should not affect me, she can talk to whoever she wants. But it is affecting me. Why?

"No rudra you can't come here" she told him.

"WHYYYYYY" that bivth said more like whined like a kid.

"Because my family's here and I can't afford to get caught by them" she explained it to him while he whined even more. I felt that sudden urge to kill him.

"Please?????" He said in a kidish tone, the hell is wrong with this man?

"Rudra will meet tomorrow na? Please?" She said in a convening manner.

"Fineeeeeeee" i heard that idiotic creature say.

"Ohk then will talk to you later byeee hubby" she said giggling before hanging up the call. And she left towards the ladies section.

I wanted how to tell me who she was talking to! I could not think about anything else so I started to follow her.

I looked around trying to find prishaThere she is, beside her sister. I looked carefully only to see her admiring a mangalsutra.

I diverted my attention towards maa as I felt her gaze on me . She looked me with the questioning gaze. To escape the situation I just casually asked,"Everything done ladies?"

"Almost" maa replied back to me with a small smile glistening over her face.I nodded walking out of there.

After half an hour~We were done.

I just got a sherwani for myself nothing more than that.We all were leaving for our respective houses just then something struck my mind and i went inside the mall again, I walked towards the ladies section, and stood in front of the reception counter.

"Excuse me, pack me the mangalsutra and that lengha" i said getting inside the store. And pointing out towards a particular lengha. And at the mangalsutra Prisha was admiring a while back.

(The lengha)

(The mangalsutra)

A while back I saw prisha admiring this mangalsutra and this lengha, so i decided to buy it.

I don't know what the actual Fvck is wrong with me. Whatever. I shrruged it off and walked outside the mall.~~~~~~~~~~~~~~~~~~~PRISHA'S POV.

"Everything done ladies?" I heard a husky voice.

I turned around only to see jiju standing beside his mother.

"Almost " aunty says before he leaves off somewhere.

Well i got my dress without any difficulty but right now i am helping di finding her dressAnd btw the wedding is in 4 days !!!!

(What prisha brought for herself)

Finally we found her dress too.But there was something that had me admiring it.It was another bridal lehenga. Huff. I will get it, the day I'll get married. Hehe. For now let's leave. I said following everyone outside the mall.~~~~~~~~~~~~~~That's it for today Ohk so my goofballs don't forget to voteAnd yeah that's it for today.Stay updated.Byeeee>>>>~~~
~~~~~~~~~~~~~
~~~~~~~~~~~~~

Chapter 8: wedding

P risha's POVIt's been 3 days since shopping.We are in Rajasthan. As di, wanted it to be an Indian royal wedding. And today's my di's wedding. Ah I can't believe she's getting married. Jiju is a nice man he'll keep her happy. Sad part Rudra won't be attending the wedding cause he had some urgent work and is out of town. Good part Abhishek is here. Well let's see if di is ready or not.

(What she is wearing)I came inside Di's room.

"Di?" I asked . finding her in her room. She wasn't in her room.

I checked the washroom thinking she's inside it.

Only to find her nowhere. I started freaking out.

I immediately rushed to find maa. ....Until now i have called everyone. Everybody is looking devastated. Maa is crying. Baba is sitting numb. While me and bhaiya are trying to contact di.

"Pri did you check if she left a letter or something?" Bhaiya asked. I shook my head and started finding out if she left something behind.

And after searching i found a note inside her study table.

"I found it " i started reading it out loud.

I am sorry everyone! I never wanted this! Never. I didn't want to get married to Abhiman. I already loved someone else. I am sorry. I am really sorry. I tried telling this to maa , but she was not ready to listen to anything she was reluctant to get me married to Abhiman. I am sorry baba, bhaiya, maa, prisha and especially Abhiman.Please don't try to find me. The time you'll get this note, I'll be gone. Far away from here. If possible then forgive me.-Sneha.

"What will we do now?" Maa asked as she broke down.

"Shut up. It's all your fault." Baba yelled at her.

"Let's first call the Rajvansh family and tell all this to them" bhaiya said and we all agreed.

Within next 5 mins everyone was present in the room.

Bhaiya narrated the whole story to them.

"WHAT IS HAPPENING HERE?" i looked behind only to see jiju standing there, anger was radiating from him.

"We all are so sorry hukum. Hame maaf kariye. Hume nahi pata tha ke sneha itna bada kadam utha legi" baba said joining his hands and keeping his pagdi onto jiju's feet.

My eyes welled up with tears looking at baba begging him. I'll never forgive you di. Just because of you baba has to beg infront of someone.

"What about all the media standing outside this palace? What about our reputation? Can your sorry mend this situation?" Uncle said trying to suppress his anger.

"I have a solution " maa said blankly looking at jiju.

"We can get prisha married with Abhiman " she said while more tears welled up in my eyes.

"Aunty how can you do-" Abhishek tried saying something but I held his hand and shook my head indicating him to not say anything at the moment.

"Ohk" jiju exclaimed before walking out of the room. How can he say that? He was supposed to marry my sister not me! Why did he agree on this?

"I am sorry meri bacchi but please do us a favour please get married to Abhiman." Baba pleaded. before walking out of the room followed by maa.

"No please no. Bhaiya please don't do this. Please." I spoke, fear took a hold of my mind and heart.

Bhaiya" i cried my heart out instead of saying anything he engulfed me in a hug.

"I am sorry baccha. I can't do anything. I am helpless. they are way more influential than we are" I cried more and more. My heart ached very badly. I love rudra so much. I can't do this to him. I can't do this to myself I can't do this to US. I was disturbed when a maid knocked on the door.

"Yeh lengha hukum ne bhejwaya hai," she said and kept it on the dressing table.

"Bacha you need to get ready" bhaiya exclaimed while he himself teared up.

"No bhaiya please no" i pleaded choking onto my own tears. He just pecked my forehead before leaving me with alone Abhishek. As soon as bhaiya left Abhi hugged me.

"Abhi please stop this. I love Rudra. I can't do this to him. He loves me Abhi. Please Abhi." He cried with me before leaving me alone. While I got ready. ~~~~~~~ABHIMAN'S POV

I was getting ready. Maa recived a call and she rushed out of the room. Followed by everyone.

I too went behind them. Only to find out that Sneha was missing. DAMMIT.

"WHAT IS HAPPENING HERE?" i screamed in my Stern and thick accent.

"We are sorry hukum. Hame maaf kariye. Hume nahi pata tha ke sneha itna bada kadam utha legi" Sneha's father said joining his hands and keeping his pagdi onto my feet .

"What about all the media standing just outside this palace? What about our reputation? Can your sorry mend this situation?" Dad said trying to suppress his anger.

"I have a solution " Sneha's mom exclaimed blankly looking at me. I waited for her to complete her sentence.

"We can get prisha married to Abhiman " she said earning gasps in return, my gaze automatically went towards prisha only to find her eyes filled with warm tears.

"Aunty how can you do-" that guy from earlier at the fest, whom she hugged tried saying something but she held his hand and shook her head indicating him to not say anything at the moment.

My heart clenched seeing her tears. I myself didn't knew why so?

Not able to see her tears i replied to her mother back with a quick "ohk" before walking out of the room. Followed by my family.

One thing is sure. I am in love. I've never acted this way before.

"It wasn't her fault beta " maa tried to defend prisha.

"I know" i spoke calmly.

"Then-" I cut her off in between.

"Start the preparations" i spoke in my authoritative voice while everyone sighed. They know better not to object my decisions.

Remembering something I called a maid, She came and waited for me to say something "give this lengha to prisha" i ordered her, she nodded while bowing at me before leaving.

It was the lengha that she wanted.

~~~~~~~~~~~~~~~~~~~~~~~Prisha's POV

I got ready. To my surprise the lengha was the one that I saw earlier at the mall.

(The lengha)

(Her look)

Bhaiya knocked on the door. Before he came inside the room. I looked at him with silent tears flowing out of my eyes.

"It's time kiddo" he said and i nodded, accepting my fate. I was about to get up..when my phone rang.

It flashed "Rudra " and that's it my tears started flowing like anything.

I switched off my phone with my shivering hands. My mind flashed all the memories we created together. It broke my heart.
~~~~~~~~~~~~~~~~~~~~~~~

Bhaiya came and held my hand in a reassuring manner before guiding me out of the room.

Author's POV

Abhiman sat down at his place, waiting for his bride.

Just after a few minutes, the bride came with a veil covering her face, looking so beautiful with her red bridal lehenga. She looked ethereal. As she stepped down the stairs, Abhiman looked at her fluttered. His heart did backflips.

Kritika went to Prisha's side and made her sit beside Abhiman.

The priest started the mantra and rituals of the wedding. A fire is burning in the center of the mandap. the couple stood up for JAI MALA . First the bride puts the jai mala around the neck of her groom then the groom does the same. Slowly Kanyadan's time came and Prisha's parents came to perform this ritual. And now it was for saat Phera...(Seven circles around sacred fire Saat Phere are seven vows taken collectively by the bride and the groom as they do the parikrama around Agni Dev by taking him as a witness to their marriage. This is called AgniSakhi. The groom leads his bride while doing the first four parikramas while the latter leads her man during the remaining three pheres.)

The couple stood up. The groom has to take the first four phera followed by the bride who takes the remaining three. Abhiman grabbed prisha's hands. Tear left from her eyes.

In the first round or phera, the couple prays to God for plenty of nourishing and pure food. They pray to God to let them walk together so that they will get food.

In the second round or phera, the couple prays to God for a healthy and prosperous life. They ask for physical, spiritual and mental health from God.

In the third phrra, the couple prays to God for wealth. They ask God for the strength for both of them so that they can share the happiness and pain together. Also, they pray so that they can walk together to get wealth.

In the fourth round, the couple prays to God for the increase in love and respect for each other and their respective families.

In the fifth round, the bride and groom together pray for the beautiful, heroic and noble children from God.

In the sixth round around the fire, the couple asks for a peaceful long life with each other.

In the final seventh round, the couple prays to god for companionship, togetherness, loyalty and understanding between themselves. They ask God to make them friends and give them the maturity to carry out the friendship for a lifetime. The husband says to his new wife that now they have become friends after the Seven Vows/Saat Phere and they will not break their friendship in life.

(I didn't knew about any of these rituals , i just found this on Google, i apologise if I Missed something, or wrote something wrong)

Now after the seven steps, Pandit ji tells the groom to place the Mangalsutra around the bride's neck. Abhiman took the mangalsutra and leaned in towards prisha, to tie it around her neck.

(Mangalsutra:- A nuptial chain : necklace with black beads in it.)

Later on pandit ji tells him to apply the sindoor sindoor (Vermillion) at the partition of the bride's hair. Abhiman pulls up the veil of Prisha and in the process his eyes met those hazel ones. He applied the sindoor without breaking the eye contact.

Pandit ji announced them as husband and wife and instructs them to take the blessing of elders.

It was now time for the vidai.

Prisha cried holding onto her baba. "Meri guddiya aapne khyal rakh Lena theek hai?" Prisha's baba tells her and she nods her head.

"Jamai sa mein bohot pyar karta hoon meri bacchi se. Bohot pyar se baba Kiya hai ise, iska khyal rakhna" prisha's baba said joining his hands.

"She isn't just your daughter anymore she is now the queen of Rajasthan too, So of course I'll take care of MY QUEEN." Abhiman tells looking at prisha.

"Khush rahiye" prisha's baba blesses both of them.Prisha walked near her brother.

"Jaa Rahi hai Bhai ki pari ?" Her brother asked her, having warm tears filled in his eyes.

"Haan" she replies back to her brother and her brother engulfs her in a tight hug.

"Apna khoob Sara dhyan rakhna ok? And baccha remember I am just a call away" she nodded her head before her brother placed gently a kiss on her forehead.

Moving forward she goes towards Abhishek and he just hugged her tightly and started crying loudly. VERY LOUDLY.

"Mujhe lag raha hai ki ye meri vidai nahi Teri hai" prisha said chuckling, trying to lighten up the atmosphere.

"Tu Jaa Rahi hai ab mein kisko sathunga? Ab mujhe kon daante ga? Ab mere sath movies kon dekhega? Ab mera sath random songs par vibe kon karega? Ab kon mera sath fictional characters par simp karenga ? Mat Jaa na pri?"he said still sobbing.

" you can meet me anytime you want Abhi. It's not like I am dyin-" she got cut off in between by Abhiman"dare you to complete the sentence wifey"

Abhiman whispered huskily in his deep and thick accent.

"Mein jaa rahi hoon apna khyal rakhiyo" prisha said hugging him before leaving with Abhiman.

~~~~~~~~~~Lemme tell you i cried my eyes out while writing prisha's POV □□Rudra didn't deserve this(ik) But as i said before in the introduction, it's going to be a love triangle. That's it for today Ohk so my goofballs don't forget to voteAnd yeah that's it for today Stay updated.Byeeee>>>>
~~~~~~~~~~

Chapter 9: wedding night

‐‐

Prisha's POVI cried all the way to this room. The marriage was inside the Mahal itself. After the vidai, i was welcomed very warmly in the house. Everybody is so sweet here that i nearly cried. Swallowing all the emotions I'm feeling i sat in the centre of jiju-shit no hukum's bed.

I am settled in his room or should I say my or our room. Gosh!, this feels so terrible.Tears welled up in my eyes again. I harshly brushed them away from my face but they shamelessly kept falling down. At this point I was literally sobbing.

The fact that I have always dreamt of being Mrs. Rudra ranawat, but here I am sitting in someone's room with his name behind mine. I don't know what to expect. I feel so angry at myself what will I answer rudra ? I betrayed him. My heart is purely filled with this bitter feeling called "guilt"

I decided to distract myself from my thoughts and got up and started looking around the room. I must say he has some really good taste. The room was way bigger than my old home. His room was giving royally Vibes. You idiot it's literally a palace what do you even expect?

I looked around and There was a big balcony with a swing attached to it. OH MY GOOODDD!! A swing. I screamed in excitement. I went there and started swinging on it. I was swinging myself forgetting all the shits that happened barely an hour ago. That's when I heard a clearing of throat. Oh holy mother..

I looked up to find him standing there, he had this sinister smirk over his face. Oh holy heaven. He stood there, he chuckled softly at my shocked face. Bhagwan jii !! Ye mere sath hi kyun hota hai. Karvali beizzati padh Gaya sukun? I thought.

I was so lost in my thoughts that I didn't notice when he was already standing in front of me. As the realisation hit, I looked up into his eyes, not being able to meet his eyes, I turned my head down.I even started counting the lil patterns in my lengha.

"Mujhe nahi pata tha, apni suhagrat ki itni excitement hogi ki aap bachon ki tarah is swing par khelne lag jayengi.

He said in his husky voice with a little amusement in it.

He took another step forwardleaving no space between us. "Waise Rani saheba Umar toh aapki bache karne ki lagti hai. Bachon ki tarah khelne ki nahi.

I looked at him with confusion when it suddenly hit me. This man! Arghhhhhhhh! For holly mother's sake I am just 21 and kids at this age? Oh sorry i forgot this is Rajasthan.

My eyes went wide and my cheeks went the darkest shade of pink. "Nahi, nahi hum sacchi mein yaha nahi bethna chahste the voh excitement mein- Not able to speak because of his brutal stare at me i shut my eyes close. Aaj hi hona tha ye sab! I thought.

When a husky chuckle made me open my eyes.

"Aren't you tired Rani saheba? " To which I just shook my head in no. He kinda looked kinda amused.

He raised his eyebrow "then wanna sit outside for a while?", and I nodded my head.

And we both took our seats on the swing keeping a little distance. Bhagwan jii? Ye kis awkward situation mein daal Diya mujhe. Mujhe toh laga tha jiju-shit sorry ! sorry! hukum gussa karenge.Par ye itne shant kyun beithe hai? Bhagwan ye kahi aane Wale tuffan se pehle ki Shanti toh nahi?Let me ask him or my overthinking self won't let me be at peace.

"Ummm can I ask you something?" I asked being hesitant.

"Hmmmm" he just hummed.

"Aren't you gonna ask me about what happened an hour ago? Or won't you yell at me or hit me-

"First of all why would I hit MY WIFE ? nobody dares to hurt the queen of Rajasthan not even myself and second of all you aren't at fault so why would I yell at you ? And don't forget that I am a king myself and a real king doesn't punish the innocent souls. He said looking at my soul . My eyes contained warm tears inside them. not knowing what to say I just kept my head down and just nodded. He lifted my chin i looked at him with my teary eyes. I swear I saw his eyes darkening.

"Why are you crying?" He asked ever so slowly gently. Bhagwan jii ! I can't love him. How can I tell him that i love someone else ? HOW?.

" If you are crying thinking about what happened a while ago then Dont please. i know it isn't for you to just randomly get paired up with a person you don't know a thing about. I know it's not going to be easy for you to get used to all this, but I will not force you on a thing, you get to wear what you want, you get to live like you desire, it's going to be a hell of a tough task, But you have me ok?"my eyes welled up with his words. Never in my life have I had someone who'll say this to me. I remember the time when I moved in with baba and maa I was just too alone. And that's it my tears started flowing from my eyes.

"Hey...kya hua aapko?" He said taking my soft hands in his rough ones.

W-What if I sa-y tha-t I can ne-ver love you? I said still sobbing.

"I'll love you enough to make this relationship work ! The only thing I'll ask from your side is nothing but loyalty. He said and he's voice was coming out very dark. I again nodded my head.

"Words biwi. Words." He said making me look up at him.

"Yes" i replied using my words as he asked.

And he just smiled a lil, looking at me obeying him.

"Bohot raat hogai hai. Let's sleep." He exclaimed as he was about to get up, I spoke.

"But mujhe abhi neend nahi aa Rahi hai, i am bored." I said.

"Then let's do something" he said.

"What?" I asked getting excited.

"The deed everyone does on their wedding night." He said staring straight into my eyes. I widened my eyes. My cheeks must be looking like a tomato.

"Ah i am feeling so sleepy" i fake yawned before heading inside the room.

Getting inside i looked at the bed and it was covered with rose petals.

I widened my eyes and looked behind only to find hukum staring at me.

"Are you gonna sleep in your bridal attire?" He asked looking confused.

"Well i don't have an option" i replied shrugging my shoulder.

"You can go inside my wardrobe, you can wear anything from my clothes, until then I'll take care of this" he spoke referring to the bed, the bed was decorated with many beautiful flowers. I remembered it's my first night.

"Ohk" saying this i went inside the. wordrobe and OMG

It was too beautiful to even exist.

After Admiring it for a while I started going through his clothes. I just need a shirt or a hoodie, cause I am already wearing shorts beneath my lengha.

After a few mins of struggle, i found A white shirt . White! My fav colour! I got rid of my clothes. I took a breath of relief.

And after that i started removing my makeup, and then coming up to my heavy jewelry. Finally I was done! I huffed.

(His shirt on her)

It's so big on me. But It looks kinda cute. It smells exactly like how he did a while ago when I was on the balcony with him.i came back to the room, only to find it all near and clean. I smiled.

He was sitting on the bed busy on his phone. I looked around to find that everything was clean . There was not a single rose petal on the bed . I mentally praised him. I was still standing on my tracks looking at the king size bed placed in the middle. How am I gonna share a bed with him?

" You should sleep. Or do you want to do the deed?" I widened my eyes hearing him say this.

He chuckled at my reaction and went back to bed on the left side.

Trying to process everything about whatever happened. I still can't digest the fact that I am married. I won't cry now, i have cried enough. Sighing I went to the other side and Layed down on my side of the bed i choose for myself, I was trying to sleep as I knew sleep wouldn't be anywhere near me tonight , cause my precious "chiku" isn't here.

After an hour~

For the past one hour I have been trying to sleep. I kept tossing and turning around.

"Aren't you able to sleep?" I flinched as I heard him say.

"Ye-ah" i said as i turned to face him.

"Any problem?" He asked facing me, he was now looking at me.

"Well-uhh-voh" i wasn't able to say it, it's embarrassing.

"What is it?" He asked

"Wellihaveahabbitofsleepingwithmystufftoyandicantsleepwithouthim" i saidfastly being embarrassed of my childish habit.

"Great ! now try saying it slowly " he asked calmly.

"Well i have a habit of sleeping with my stuff toy and i can't sleep without him" i said more like mumbled lowering my eyes. He was close to me so he heard it .

"I can be your stuff toy. Mold me in anyway you want. I am officially yours you can make anything out of me " He said and i Blushed hard over his statement.

"Come here" he said

"Huh?" I asked but before that he pulled me towards him my my waist.

"Don't think too much. Sleep. Good night Rani saheba." He said and my body acted on his words i closed my eyes and drifted into my Dreamland.

~~~~~~~~~~~~~~~~~This is it for todayNew chapter is hereeeeeeeee Goofballs Abhiman's POV will be posted once you all complete the vote target. Lemme know how it was?Don't forget to vote!!!!!Vote target 40 !!I'll upload the next chapter once the target is done Byeeeeeeee my Goofballs
~~~~~~~~~~~~~~~~~

Chapter 10:Wedding night pt.2

Tumhein sajne sawarne ki zaroorat hi nahi, Tum pe sajti hai sadgi bhi kisi zewar ki tarah.________________________

Abhiman's POV

Gosh! She looked so ethereal today when I saw her entering the mandap i lost it. I kept staring at her. Well all thanks to her sister. I am going to forgive her sister. Only because of her ,I was able to marry prisha. Well for now let's go to my biwi. I went to my room only to find those monsters there by monster, I meant Yash, Kiara, dharya.

"What do you all want?"i asked raising my eyebrows.

"Looks like someone is getting impatient, huh?" Yash asked and i rolled my eyes

"Ahem, so coming straight to the point we want money or else we won't let you get in your room" Kiara said. Oh so these monsters are here for money. I already saw this coming. It's a ritual

"And we won't take a penny less than 1 lac-" i cut Yash off by giving him a blank cheque with my signature on it. Their jaw dropped.

"Have fun and let me have fun too" i said walking inside my room"

I walked inside the room only to find the room empty. I frowned. Where is she ? I thought.

I looked around and finally went to the balcony. There she is. She looked like a child while swinging on the swing. Ohh fuckkkkkkkkkkkkkkkkkk she looks so adorable. Control Abhiman. Control. I went towards her and she didn't realise it.

"Mujhe nahi pata tha, apni suhagrat ki itni excitement hogi ki aap bachon ki tarah is swing par khelne lag jayengi. I asked teasingly in my husky voice.

Her head snapped up with a jolt.

I took another step forwardleaving no space between us. "Waise Rani saheba Umar toh aapki bache karne ki lagti hai. Bachon ki tarah khelne ki nahi. I said

She looked at me with confusion, didn't she get it?.

Her eyes went wide and her cheeks went the darkest shade of pink.

She was Not able to speak because of my intense gaze at her . She shut her eyes close. I Chuckled at her innocence. Oh how I want to fuck this innocence out of her.

"Aren't you tired Rani saheba? " i asked To which she just shook her head in no. Isn't she tired with all the things that happened today? I looked at her in amusement.

I raised my eyebrow "then wanna sit outside for a while?", and she again nodded her head. Can't she use that pretty voice of her's?

And we both took our seats on the swing keeping a little distance. I swear to god. I want to close all the distance that is between us. My chain of thought was broken when i heard her honey-like voice.

"Ummm can I ask you something?" She asked being hesitant.

"Hmmmm" i just hummed. Controlling the urge to kiss her.

"Aren't you gonna ask me about what happened an hour ago? Or won't you yell at me or hit me- I cut her off. How can she even think that I am going to hit her? I'll be dammed if I let someone or even myself hit her.

"First of all why would I hit MY WIFE ? nobody dares to hurt the queen of Rajasthan not even myself and second of all you aren't at fault so why would I yell at you ? And don't forget that I am a king myself and a real king doesn't punish the innocent souls. I said looking into her soul . To which she just kept her head down and just nodded.

I lifted her chin and she looked at me with her teary eyes. My eyes darkened. "Why are you crying?" I asked ever so slowly gently. I didn't knew that tone even existed.

"If you are crying thinking about what happened a while ago then Dont please. i know it isn't for you to just randomly get paired up with a person you don't know a thing about. I know it's not going to be easy for you to get used to all this, I know that your sister was the one supposed to marry me, but I will not force you on a thing, you get to wear what you want, you get to live like you desire, it's going to be a hell of a tough task, But you have me ok?" Her eyes weld up with tears making me panic.

"Hey...kya hua aapko?" I said taking her soft hands into my rough ones.

W-What if I sa-y tha-t I can ne-ver love you? She said still sobbing. And my eyes darkened even more. So does she love someone else? Well I don't care now. She is mine and ONLY mine.

"I'll love you enough to make this relationship work ! The only thing I'll ask from your side is nothing but loyalty. I said and my voice came out pretty dark. She again nodded her head. Getting annoyed i said

"Words biwi. Words."

"Yes" she replied back, i love her man.

And i just smiled a lil. I love the way she obeys me

"Bohot raat hogai hai. Let's sleep." I said

"But mujhe abhi neend nahi aa Rahi hai, i am bored." She said pouting. Fuck I am getting hard.

"Then let's do something" i said

"What?" She asked getting excited

"The deed everyone does on their wedding night." I said staring straight into her eyes. She widened her eyes.

"Ah i am feeling so sleepy" she fake yawned before heading inside the room. I wasn't joking.

Getting inside she looked at the bed and it was covered with rose petals.

She widened her eyes. And turned around.

"Are you gonna sleep in your bridal attire?" I asked

"Well i don't have an option" she said shrugging her shoulder

"You can go inside the wardrobe, you can wear anything from my clothes, until then I'll take care of this" i spoke referring to the bed.

"Ohk" she said and went to the wardrobe While I started cleaning the bed.

After a few mins I was done. I decided to scroll down my Instagram.

She came back wearing one of my favourite shirts.

But am i complaining? No absolutely not. She looked like a treat to my eyes.

She was just staring at the bed. I guess she's thinking how'll she sleep with me.

" You should sleep or do you want to do the deed? I said making her eyes go wide.

I chuckled at her reaction. And she went to the other side, and lay down there.

After an hour~

For the past one hour I could feel her tossing and turning around.

"Aren't you able to sleep?" I asked her turning to face her.

"Ye-ah" she replied, making me raise my eyebrows.

"Any problem?" I asked, facing her.

"Well-uhh-voh" she wasn't able to say it, i sighed.

"What is it?" i asked her once again hoping she would tell it to me.

"Wellihaveahabbitofsleepingwithmystufftoyandicantsleepwithouthim" she exclaimed . I didn't get a word out of it.

"Great ! now try saying it slowly " i said calmly.

"Well i have a habit of sleeping with my stuff toy and i can't sleep without him" she said more like mumbled lowering her beautiful eyes.

"I can be your stuff toy. Mold me in anyway you want. I am officially yours you can make anything out of me " i said calmly making her go red . From now on her red cheeks are my favourite thing about her.

"Come here" i said. Knowing how she is she'll never hug me so now I've to take matters into my own hands.

"Huh?" She asked but before that i pulled her towards me by her waist.

"Don't think too much. Sleep. Good night Rani saheba." I said and she closed her eyes and drifted into her Dreamland.~~~~~~~~~~~~~~~~~This is it for todayThe new chapter is hereeeeeeeee Goofballs One thing that is you all are just reading and are not voting. If you all complete the vote target then only I'll be posting the next chapter.Lemme know how it was?Don't forget to vote!!!!!Vote target 40 !!I'll upload the next chapter once the target is done Byeeeeeeee my Goofballs

Chapter 11: Pehli rasoi

_______________________________________Jeene bhi nahi degiMarne bhi nahi degiUski muskurahatEk din hamari Jaan hi legi..________

____

Prisha's POVLight was peaking through the window on my face. When i heard the noise of water running. i slowly opened my eyes. I looked at the wall which had a huge clock in it.

I lower my gaze only two immediately lifted up and stay at the clock once again. That was when I realised where I was. It was already 10:45. Holy mother I'm late.

Without wasting another second i jumped out of the bed and went straight to the closet. Only to find a very handsome man in his pants looking at me with a sinister smirk. not any men but my HUSBAND. The water droplets made their way to his well built up abs. Ikept staring at his abs until he cleared his throat... Pri you should write a book on how to embarrass yourself... My chain of thoughts were broken when he pulled me by my waist.

"don't worry, you can stare at me meri jaan. I am rightfully yours" his words left me with a deep shade of red...

Wo-h i wasn't sta-rting there was uhh a mosquito. Yeah a mosquito. I said smiling nervously.

"Sure" he said and left chuckling.

Arghhhhhhhh it's so embarrassing.

I wore a saree. And pairing it with a kamrbandh. My luggage came this morning. I quickly did my hair and applied my primer and then a light weighted moisturizer followed by my sunscreen and later on I decided to put on a lipstick along with a little bit of blush, and how can I forget the Love of my Life? my jhumka. I looked over the mirror , my subconscious told me that I was missing out on something and that's when I realized that I am actually MARRIED now and I have to apply Sindoor too.

"I'll do it" hukum's voice made me turn around.

He said and came forward and took the sindoor daan in his hands. Taking a pinch, he applied it. A bit of it fell on my nose.

"I'll do it everyday ok?" He asked in his deep thick accent.

"Ohk" i said nodding my head.

"We should go down now" he said And i nodded my head before going downstairs.

~~~~~~~~Downstairs~

"Good morning" hukum said followed by me.

Everybody greeted us back.

"Beta do you know that today's your pehli rasoi?" Aunty asked. Oh holy mother i forgot about this.

"Yes aunty" I replied to her back.
~~~~~~~~

"First of all don't call me aunty consider me like your mother only. Call me what you used to call your mom" she said smiling towards me.

"My mom?" I asked and i could feel my eyes getting watery. It's been years since my mother passed away and when aunty told me to call her by what I used to call my mother brought me nostalgia.

"Yes beta" she confirmed lovingly.

"Mumma?" I called out for her only to receive a cheerful and lovely smile from her.

"That's like my daughter" she exclaimed and hugged me.

"So then let's get done with the cooking?" She said pulling out of the hug and i nodded. And we went to the kitchen.

"Beta you don't have to cook all the dishes just making the sweet dish will be okay" she said and i smiled before nodding my head.

"Beta I know it must've been hard for you. You are still young. You must've had dreams. And we all just broke all of your dreams. But Ladoo (a pet name for girls used mainly in Rajasthan) remember we will never stop you from achieving your dreams. We all don't hate you or something. We will support you and your dreams. We just want one thing in return. Will you give it to us? She said and i nodded my head a few tears fell from my eyes.

"Beta please never leave my son." She said having tears in her eyes too.

"Mumma-" i was cut of in between.

"Please beta" she pleaded.

"I'll never leave him" i told her at that moment only I knew what I felt. I felt like a complete betrayer. A liar. A cheater. I felt guilty for Rudra. My life has turned into a complete mess. As I spoke those words she engulfed me in a hug.

After a minute or so she pulled out from the hug and started instructing me as of where the things that I might need while cooking.

"Ohk then there are the things you might need" she said pointing towards a certain shelf.

"I am leaving , if you need any help I am always there " saying this she left. Making me burst into the tears I was holding on earlier. I can't love him. I love Rudra. I can't betray this family. I just cannot love him. I will tell all this to hukum today itself.

I wiped my tears away, and started making kheer.

After half an hour~

The kheer is done. I called out for the house helpers to take the kheer out with them to the dining table.

At the dining table~

I was settled beside hukum,Everybody was almost done with their break-fast.

Now it's time for the kheer. Yash took the first spoon of it in his mouth.

I was fidditting the end of my saree's pallu.

"Bhabhiiiiiiiiii-saaa" i heard Yash yell.

"What happened? Is the kheer too sweet? Is it too plain? Is it-"

"shhhh" hukum shussed me back to my seat.

"Bhabhi sa can you come here?" He asked and everybody looked at him being confused. Nevertheless I got up from my place and went towards him.

"Can you give me your hand?" He asked and i gave my hand to him.

He turned my hand, and kissed my knuckles.

"I am clearly in love with this kheer of yours" he exclaimed with a wide smile over his face.

"You scared me , badmaash " i told him keeping my hand over my heart. And he giggled with everyone else.

Everybody enjoyed the kheer. And gave me gifts. I refused at first but after A LOT of convincing, i accepted it.

After the gift distribution we all went to our respective rooms.

Currently I am standing in hukum-our room.

"Do you want to say something?" He asked noticing me staring at him.

"Ah..voh...hum-" i shuttered and as usual i was cut off in between.

"Jo khena hai saaf saaf kahiye mohtarma" he told me, solely paying atten-tion to what I was about to say.

"Hum-hum ki-si or s-e mo-ha-bbat kartey hein" i said keeping my gaze on the floor.

"Hum jaante hei" he replied ever so calmly. Making my head shoot up.

"Huh?"i said not believing what just entered inside my holy ears.

"I said i know that you love someone else. And as we are married now it doesn't matter. Now let me clear something. You are standing in front of me. Claimed AS MINE. The past doesn't matter. And Rani saheba the things that are mine are ONLY MINE. Nobody dares to look at you the way I do. And I won't appreciate you saying you love someone else in front of me. I won't force you in any sort of relationship neither I will stop you from falling in love with me. Get this information inside your tiny little head" he said gently yet it radiated a scary aura. It felt like the calm before the storm.

"What-i mean I still love Rudra. I love him hukum. This isn't right. I can't leave him-" i my mouth instantly shut down as I felt his index finger over my lips.

"I like when you talk. I like hearing this honey-filled voice of yours. But i would appreciate it more if you talk about me not about some other men who aren't me. And i want no arguments on this topic" He said with his finger still on my lips. i just nodded my head feeling scared.

"I will be in my study room. If you want something come straight to my cabin." He said before leaving.

And i let my tears fall free, that I've been holding on. I went toward the bed and hid my face in a pillow sobbing my heart out. "I am not a cheater rudra. I am not. Please forgive me for this. If I could have the courage to stop this i would have done it. I am sooo sorry Rudra." I mumbled between my sobs, After crying for some good hours i fell asleep.________________

________________________That's it for today Feeling bad for rudra & prisha Ohk so my goofballs don't forget to voteAnd yeah that's it for today Stay updated.Byeeee>>>>

Chapter 12: her nightmares

We crossed 1k yayyyy (i cried) So to celebrate it.... a early update for my goofballs□_____________________________Gulaab jesi ho aap, gulaab Lgti ho Halka sa muskura do lajawab Lgti ho.______________ ______________Author's POVHe came back into their room completing his work only to find her sleeping peacefully.He looked at the time it was already 1: 23 am. he sighed. And went to change his clothes.

Abhiman's POV

I streched my arms letting out a yawn. Closing my laptop. I did some streching. I know i shouldn't have left her in the room alone like the way I did. But the Idea of her loving someone else who's not me didn't settle well with me.I love her. And i won't lose the women i love this time. I won't. Even if i would have to fight with the whole damm world. I don't give a fuck about anything. She's mine and ONLY mine.

I came back only to find her sleeping peacefully.

I looked at the time it was already 1: 23 am. I sighed. And went to change my clothes.

I went to the wordrobe only to find all her clothes scattered around the floor. I shook my head. And neatly arranged all her things. The time I was done I was sweating. And then i decided to go take a shower.

After 20 mins~I came back only and i was walking towards prisha to plant a kiss on her forehead. I know it's inappropriate to kiss her without her consent but I guess itna toh chalta hai. I muffled a laugh and shook my head.

The scene before my eyes left me in shock.

Prisha was fvcking TREMBLING while mumbling something.

"Don't do this please. I beg you please" she pleaded choking onto her tears. She kept mumbling it.

"Prisha wake up meri jaan what happened?" I said while shaking her a Little bit.

After trying for several times i decided to sprinkle some water on her face . And she woke up with a jerk. I sat beside her.

"What happened bacha- i was cut off when she hugged me suddenly. She cried and cried. Making my heart rip apart into peices. I don't know who is responsible for this condition of hers but i swear if i found him or her I'll make them regret their existence.

"Shhh mera baccha. I am here. With you. Always. Tell me the name and you'll find him 10 feet down the ground." I cooed her gently taking her on my lap. But she just hid her face into my neck and sobbed badly that her whole damm body trembled.

"You know one thing? Gulaab jesi ho aap, gulaab Lgti ho Halka sa muskura do lajawab Lgti ho." She sniffed more by hearing my words. Fvck this isn't going anywhere.

"If I could take all the pain from your heart and pour it into mine, I would. What can I do for you meri jaan? Tell me ?" She didn't replied anything and sobbed more making my heart sink to my stomach.

"Bacha this is not how it works. You know right i am here for you?I asked gently moving my fingers in her brown lucious locks. She lifted her her head up from my neck. And nodded still crying.

"Will you tell me what are you feeling? Or what was the thing that made you cry?" I asked patting her back to help her reduce her hiccups so she could speak properly.

"I ca-n't des-crib-e ho-w I fe-el right n-ow" she said sobbing.

"Throw the words out I'll put them together." I told her, removing the hairs dangling over her face.

"I'm bad with words" She said, staring at me with her tears spilling eyes.

"I'm good at reading eyes" I replied wiping her tears that were flowing from her eyes.

"Shh, calm down. I am here and I will not let anyone harm you. Now, stop crying." I told her while rubbing her back gently.

She wraps her hands around my neck tightly and cries softly. But I didn't stop rubbing her back. Just a few minutes later I hear her breathing softly indicating that she has fallen asleep. Not wanting to disturb her So, I very gently lay her down on the bed before covering half of her body with the comforter.I planted a soft kiss on her forehead before looking at her tear stained face.

"Hurt Is the word I am feeling right now. Nobody could make me feel this and I know nobody can do, other than prisha."

"I won't force you to share the thing that is troubling you, but the day you come to me and says the name of the person who is responsible for your this state will be found 10 feet under the ground. I don't know what's bothering you or what you're so scared of. But I know one thing for sure that I will not let anything happen to you. I will make sure to love you like the way you desire, the way you want with the exact amount of it and the amount will depend on me."I let out these words unconsciously looking at her sleeping form. ____Ik it's short but i swear I'll make it up to you all. It's just my mind was kinda messed up. That's it for today.What do you think is the reason behind her nightmares?And why are you all not voting huh? My goofballs are getting spoiled huh? Ok then I won't update this until i have at least 40 votes

Chapter 13: Bullies

"Ishq mein inteha nahi to ishq mein kya maza?Inteha mein ishq nahi toh inteha se kya maza?"
~Ain_______________________________________Prisha's POVIt's already been 3 days since the nightmare incident and I am still avoiding talking to Hukum.

Ik i should tell this to hukum he has the right to know about my past Yet, I am scared to recall the most horrible part of my life. So, I am going to wait for the correct time, and then I will reveal everything.

Everything aside, I have gotten close to Yash Kiara and dharya. Especially Yash devar sa. He reminds me of rishab Bhaiya. And Kiara, she reminds me of Sneha di. And about Dharya devar sa, he's the most caring one yet the most practical one.

I have asked hukum to let me go to the college. And he agreed to it without any hesitation.

I am RN getting ready for my college. Today's my first day in this new college. Sadly I don't have Abhi beside me. He was my personal cheerleader and supported me in my both bad and good decisions I took in my life. I kinda miss him. It's not like we don't talk anymore. We do. But I want him here. Pehla din hai Kanha ji! bacha Lena.

I heard a horn indicating that hukum is waiting outside for me. I prayed for the last time before heading out.

I settled down in his car. And he drove off.

There's heavy traffic outside. I looked outside and I saw a child selling "gajray"

"I wanna buy them" i mumbled while pouting.

"Wait for me I am coming in a while" he says and i nodded my head at him.

He goes in the direction of that kid who was selling gajray and i could see him buying a pair of gajray. He came back. And settle down on his place. And lifted the gajray in the air.

"Can I ?" He asked indicating that he wants to tie those gajray on my hair.

"You can" saying this i giggled because this is actually cute... I so wanted to have this kinda moment in my life and it's happening today.

As i turned around i could feel his hands doing their work on my hairs. But I could feel him struggling with it.

And the next moment I felt hot breaths over my neck . Indicating that he is closer to me. My heart sank to my stomach.

"Done!" He exclaimed as soon as he was done.

"Tha-nk you" i managed to say while shuttering.And he showed me his hundred watt smile.

"He should smile more often" i thought having absolutely no control over my mind.

"If that is so, you should know that you are the reason behind it." he said making my eyes go wide. Did I say that out loud? I thought.

"Very loud" he said making me more embarrassed. The rest of the ride was spent in silence.

After 15 mins~

He opened the car's door for me, and i stepped out of the car,

"Yash will be around here. If you have any problems then inform it to him he'll take care of it" He said and i nodded my head And he left before giving me his smile.

I started walking into the entrance of the college...i slowly walked into the corridor of the college keeping my gaze down. I bumped into someone and I lifted my gaze up. Only to find that I bumped into a girl. She had a whole group standing a step behind her.

"I-I-I-----am sor-ry" i shuttered.

"Aww look at this cutie here. Cute isn't she?" That girl said while touching my hair.

"Please leave me" i said as my sixth sense told me that they are definitely going to rag me.

"Not so early sweetheart, Meet me after the classes in front of the girls washroom." She spoke as i nodded.

"Ji" i answered her, while all of them left.

After the classes ended i stood in front of the washroom where that group was waiting for me.

I was standing in front of them with my eyes hung low.

"Naam?" The girl from earlier asked.

"Prisha" i looked at them, they had this sinister smirk over their faces.

The girl in front of me scoffed sarcastically.

"Look at her dress, itne bade college mein iss behen ji ko entry kisne di?" Another girl said coming closer to me.

" Humein Jane de Hume late ho raha hai" She excused herself and was ready to leave but one of them grabbed her arm and dragged her to the floor throwing her on it. Prisha whimpered when the leader of that group tightly clutched my hair.

"Stop being a bivth, let us enjoy sometime with you" She cussed letting go of her hairs

I gasped when she snatched my dupatta and passed it to another girl and she threw that dupatta on floor.

"Bhai ye toh baccho ki tarah rone bhi lag gayi" said one of them making the others laugh while i struggled taking the breath, suddenly my past started appearing infront of me, making me feel light headed.

The other one rotated my hand and pushed me on the floor, i stumbled.

"Apko kya chahiye mujhese? Jaan chode hamari! hame Jane dein" i said fearing what they might do next. And that's when a slap landed on my cheek.

" what's going on?" Yash got inside the washroom as he heard prisha's voice and watched the scene before his eyes , his eyes fell on prisha he widened his eyes with terrifying glint in them. He knew what would have happened here, because this college is famous for ragging.

" Sir?" She called out for Yash.

Caring less Yash walked towards prisha who was on the verge of having a panic attack, and hugged her gently.

"Bhabhi sa, are you okay?" He asked.

"Bhabhi?" The leader of the group asked and Yash chose to ignore her.

"D-on't wor-ry I a-m ok- she couldn't complete her words as she started having the flashbacks of her past and lost her consciousness. Making Yash'seyes wide.

"Fvck" he cursed under his breath while holding her.

"You all are so dead. If something happens to my bhabi sa then you'll know what I am capable of. And let alone that, you will regret once Bhai-sa finds this out." I said looking at them dead in their eyes.

Saying this he lifted prisha taking her to his Lambo, he laid her down on the back seat of it.

Abhiman's POV

I was in a meeting with Rishabh. I am singing a deal with him.(prisha's brother) i received a call from Yash. I frowned upon it cause he doesn't usually call me, he handles his own shit by himself, but if he does call me, then it's definitely something serious.

I excused myself and picked up the call.

"Hello?" He asked in a panic stricken voice.

"Hmm?" I asked

"Bhai sa aap Ghar jaldi se aa jayein please. Bhabhi sa behosh ho gayi hein. Hum unhe Ghar leke ja rahe hein." He said hurriedly.

"Ye kaise hua??? I asked you to take proper care of her. You have highly disappointed me. And don't take her home. Take her to a good hospital I will be there."

"What happened?" Rishabh asked noticing my worried expressions.

"Something happened to prisha!" I asked fuming in anger. Anger of the reason behind her this situation and disappointment of not protecting her.

"WHAT?" Rishabh stood up from his seat.

"I am going to check up on her" i said getting up from the seat.

"I am coming with you" he said and i nodded.

without wasting any time we rushed towards the hospital.

At the hospital~

We asked the receptionist about her room number and went to her room .There she is. Sitting on the bed zoned out.

"What the fuck is actually happened pri?" She came out of trance at the voice of her elder brother from behind, she turned around only to see her brother and then on me. We both had serious expressions on our faces. but the moment my eyes fell on her she noticed how my expressions darken, my gaze eventually fell on her face it was tears stricken all red from hours of crying and wait- was that a slap mark over her cheeks?

Abhiman got closer to her and grabbed her face gently to tilt it so he could look clear at her mark. There was rage building inside him, some- one slapped her, his wife. The queen of Rajasthan. Someone has slapped her hard enough to leave mark behind. He could not protect her. It's all Because of him. Her lips curved in pout and she burst into tears, while wrapping arms around him. This was the moment he promised that he's gonna end whoever has made her cry today. She was hiccuping badly. So badly. Abhiman clutched onto her tightly.

She cried against his chest, her sobs and every hiccup she took were making him feel something he never did. Maybe it was the pain of seeing your loved one in a miserable state.

Yash and prisha have developed a strong bond similar of brother and sister. Seeing his sister cry made his heart clench in pain. The person who has hurt his sister Is done for sure.

"Tell me exactly what happened" Abhiman asked crassing her hair softly as she pulled away and wiped tears with the back of her hand. He's only calm right now because of her.

She shook her head.

"Humara Dil betha Jaa Raha hai aapko ese dekh ke" Abhiman said moving the strand of her hair that was covering her face.

"Kuch- i shoot a glare towards her.

"K-kuch ladkiyon ne bully kiya Hume washroom mein . One of them Snatched my dupatta and slapped me they said alot of bad words too. I felt disgus-ted by their words" She told them. She said between her sobs. Abhiman had a very psychopathic look over his face. There was a really different aura coming from him . The way his eyes darkened was only saying one thing.

"Don't worry I am here na?" I assured her.

After some checkups , She got discharged and I took her to home.

At home~

"Aagaye mere bacche Ghar?" Ma asked.

"Haan maa" i replied back.

"Meri bacchi din kaisa gya aapka?" Maa asked prisha.

"Bohot accha mumma" she replied like she wasn't the one literally shivering while crying a while ago. I shook my head at her.

"Bohot badhiya" maa said.

"Jaldi se aajao. Mein khana laga deti hoon. Maa said smiling sweetly.

"Maa mujhe kuch important kaam hai. Aur aap prisha ke liye khana upar hi bhijwa dijiye" i said to which she just nodded her head.

I took prisha with me up to our room."How can you lie so effortlessly?" I said trying to act suspicious.

"Aadat hai humein" she said.

Meanwhile a maid knocked on the door. I opened it. She had a tray in her hands which had a meal inside it.

I took the tray and went towards prisha." Humein bhook nahi hai. Hum bad mein kha lenge." She tried making an excuse.

"But khana toh khana padega" i said forwarding a bite.

"Bhukh nahi hai" she said.

"Nakhre na karein Rani saheba.Hum nakhre utha lenge aapke But yeh Wale nahi" i said forwarding her a bite and thankfully she took it without further tantrums.

She was chewing it but her eyes immediately filled up with warm water. Before i could ask anything she asked....

W-hy are y-ou caring for a p-erson wh-o you we-re force-d to get marrie-d? Wh-at am I to y-ou? She asked between her sobs.

"You are not just anyone. You are MINE and I know how to take care of the things that are mine. And to answer your second question, you are the house where my heart lives." I replied wiping her tears

"Aap humse itni mohabbat kyun karte hain?" She asked looking at my eyes as if trying to find something in them.

"Wajha nahi chahiye Hume aapse pyar karne ke liye." I replied reflecting the emotion she was trying to find into my eyes.

_______________________________________That's it for today. Our Abhi-man_pyar mein pagal_Rajwansh And why are you all not voting huh? My goofballs are getting spoiled huh? Ok then I won't update this until i have at least 30 votes

Chapter 14: dealing with it

Nights will tell youThat your thoughts are there in my dream How should I forget youSince you're there in my dreams?______________________PRISHA'S POV

"Aap humse itni mohabbat kyun karte hain?" I asked looking at his eyes as if trying to find something in them.

"Wajah nahi chahiye Hume aapse pyar karne ke liye." He replied reflecting the emotion i was trying to find into my eyes.

"Am i special to you?" I asked still looking deep into his eyes.

"You are" he replied back gazing deep in my eyes.

"What's so special about me?" I asked, still not believing him.

" Agar Aap na ho toh hamarey liye kuch special nahi" he replied. The tears that built up in my eyes finally fell down. He didn't let those tears fall down instead he kissed my tears.

"Aur kuch puchna hai aapko?" He asked.

"Nahi" i replied him back. My heart was beating fastly. I don't know why.

"Then you should sleep now. You must be tired" he exclaimed while i shook my head.

"I am not tired. I am scared of the things that are going inside my mind" i said only to get engulfed in a tight hug. he hugged me, tightly. As if trying to hide me from this world.

"Now?" He asked while hugging me.

I didn't reply nor did I know what to do but i hugged him back. My heart wanted me to. And i obliged.

He pulled out of the hug and lifted me in his arms. And slowly took me towards the bed. And laid me down on it.

"If possible I'll try to fight with the demons inside that Lil brain of yours, you won't have to fight them alone. I am here. With you. For you. Always." He stated. I closed my eyes feeling safe. This was the feeling I was unknown to.

He Layed down on the other side of the bed. He pulled me closer by my waist and hugged me tightly. I could feel his heart beating fastly and mine stopping.

"Today i found my safe place" i heard my heart yelled.

And before I knew i fell asleep in his arms. ________________________AB-HIMAN'S POV

I could feel her breath getting slow. Indicating she has fallen asleep. The way she fits perfectly into my arms, like she was destined to be in it.

I kissed her forehead, before detaching myself away from her. I looked at her sleeping form for the last time before heading out of the room.

I went straight to my study room where Yash, Kiara and dharya were present.

"I hope you all might have known what had happened today" i asked in a stren voice.

"We do" all three of them answered

"So do you all realise the fact, that the things which took place today, were not supposed to happen?"

They nodded.

"So dharya, Yash and Kiara, i am leaving the bullying part to the three of you. And rest of the job is mine to do." I said. And they all nodded there head in obedience.

Saying this i left from there.I dialled Lakshay's and Aadvik's number.

"Arey mein yaad hun tujhko? Mujhe toh laga shadi ke baad mujhe bhul hi jayega." Lakshay spoke.

"Bakwas band kar aur gaur se sun" i said in serious tone, and explained what happened today.

"So what do you want us to do?" They both asked being serious this time.

"Rina. the girl that assaulted prisha is the daughter of Mr.agarwal. file a case against her. And deal with it yourself. I am trusting you on this. And Aadvik cancel all the deals with Mr.Agarwal and inform this to everyone that whoever finalizes the deal with Mr.agarwal has to face me." I told them the whole process. And ended the call.

"Whoever hurts prisha has to face me. Not the king of Rajasthan. Not the CEO of Rajwansh enterprises. But the husband of Prisha." I exclaimed recalling her crying form......_______________________________________Here's a mini update for you allI won't be uploading the chapters until Saturday.I am going to my Village and there's literally no network there.This is it for todayLemme know how it was?Don't forget to vote!!!!!Vote target 30 !!Byeeeeeeee my Goofballs~~~~~~~~~~~~~

Chapter 15 : dealing with it pt.2

No shariys for today _________________Author's POV

With rage filled up in their nerves, they steeped in the canteen. Making the students there widened their eyes, as they knew who these three were.

" step out everybody except Rina and her minions, let me also know who this Rina is" dharya's voice came out deeper and louder than expected as he entered the canteen with Yash and Kiara.

Without a word they all stepped out one by one, leaving them alone.

"Kiara mam mujhe pata nahi tha wo apki bhabhi thi ." She spoke out hurriedly out of anxiety.

"Mujhe paheliyan bujhane ki aadat nahi hein, line up." Dharya said in his dominating voice. They paired up in a line.

"Tum mein se bhabhi-sa ka dupatta kisne hath lagaya tha?" Yash asked with his gaze moving accross the three.

"Shreya did!" One of them spoke out of fear.

"Yash- i mean sir, M-mene nahi kiya! Rina did all the things!" She pointed at the leader. Sherya yelled with horrified expressions.

Yash scoffed at her stupid remark.

"Kiara hold Rina" Yash said more like demanded, he had a blade in his hands.

"Which hand did you use to touch bhabhi sa's dupatta?" Yash asked to which she didn't answered anything.

"I don't like to repeat myself, nor will I show any mercy, to any of you" Yash said.

"R-igh-t o-n-e" she replied being a shuttering mess.

Yash didn't wasted any more time and gave a big ass cut on her palm. And her gaze went to her palm dripping red in blood. She started crying like a miniac. Making Kiara chuckle out loud

"Aww already crying sweetheart? Come on sweetheart there's a lot more to come on your way." Kiara said with that evil look on her face.

"Who slapped bhabhi-sa?" Kiara asked and was looking at them with rage. Making them gulp hard.

"Niyasa did" Shreya said.

"I didn-'t kn-ew sh-e was fro-m your fa-mily " niyasa shut her mouth immediately and winced when kiara tightened her grip around her wrist. And she started wiggling under Kiara's tight grip.

Kiara went towards her and slapped her harder across the face.

"Now coming to a conclusion, i won't repeat myself, if i find any of you guys doing this shit again, you won't face us, but the husband of prisha, bhabhi-sa." Said Yash.

"I guess now you know better not to mess up with the Rajwansh family" Yash said with a sinister smile on his face.

"A word out of here, and you'll find what a living hell is." Dharya said before walking out along with Kiara and Yash.

They knew even if they dared to open their mouth they will be the one to get in trouble.

The three of them left from there completing their work.____________ __________________This is it for today ☐took my brother's hospot to upload this chapterIf possible I'll try to upload the next chapter.(if you won't vote i won't upload either)Ohkk so byeee-my Goofballs

Chapter 17 : Effect

A double update for mah goofballs ___________________Pal ek pal mein hi tham sa gya~Tu haath mein haath Jo de gya~_________________Prisha's POVHe loves me!

It was clear in his eyes! Anything or anyone can lie or blind us. But the unsaid tales the eyes tells can never lie.

But the fact of him loving me is affecting me. He has all the things a girl will desire. He is a billionaire, handsome and what not?But the thing i ever wanted from someone is love and affection. And apparently he has all the qualities.

The way he handled me when I had a nightmare.

The way he accepted me even after knowing i would never be able to love him.

The way he calmed me down.

The way he and his little actions have started affecting me.

Today I saw something in his eyes that I feared the most....LOVE.

It was so clear in his eyes that it made me scared...what if he could see through my eyes too? What if he could read my eyes only to find that his actions are affecting me?

I was so lost in my thoughts when I heard someone clearing his throat.

I looked beside me only to find hukum sitting beside me.

"Aap soyi nahi?" He asked

"Neend nahi aayi" i replied

"Koi baat Jo aapko pareshan kar rahi hein?" He asked as if reading my eyes.

"Nahi hukum- i was cut off by him

"Hukum na kahiye Hume. Biwi hai aap hamari. Haq Banta hai aapka humpe , hamara naam le sakti hein aap." He said and it would be a lie if i said i didn't melted

"Hukum- i was yet again cut off by him

"Phir Se? Abhiman. Abhiman naam hein hamara" he said and got a lil closer , he tucked a strand of my hair behind my ear. And i lowered my gaze from the intensity of his gaze.

"Abhi-m-a-an" i said

"Not like this try breaking it and then try to pronounce it. Repeat after me, Abhi-maan. Your turn." He explained

"Maan?" I said looking up in his eyes

"What did you call me?" He said

"Maan?" I repeated

"Again " he said this time closing his eyes

"Maan" i said with a slight smile on my face

"Again" he said himself smiling

"Maan. Maan. Maan" i said giggling

"Isha thank youuuuuu. You made me the happiest man alive on this earth." My eyes filled up with warm tears.

"Wh-at did you just call me?" I asked

"Didn't you like it? I am sorry ,please don't cry " he said panicking. Instead of replying i hugged him.

"You made the happiest girl alive on the earth today. Thank you for calling me that!!!" I said pulling out of the hug.

I realised what I did just now!

"I am sorry i hugged you without your consent" i apologized

"You stole the beat of my heart, the shine of my eyes, the breath in my lungs, the thoughts throughout the day. Did I complain about that? You know what ? Even after knowing how harmful it is for my heart , i would wish for nothing else but for you to steal more. He said looking deep into my eyes making me as red as a tomato!!!!

"Hum ek baar phir aapko bta rahe hein, haq hai aapka humpe. Us haq ko jatana shikhiye. He repeated gently keeping a hand of his on my either sides of cheeks. To which I just nodded my head making him smile.

"Thak gayi hongi aap. It's late we should sleep now" he said to which I nodded my head. He turned off the lights and laid on the other half of the bed.

"Come here" he said opening his arms i hesitated at first but gave up. He scooped me in his arms and gently patted my back until I fel asleep.___

_______________This one was CUTE Bro I am so proud of myself for writing this chapter So yeah this is it for today

Chapter 18: First kiss

Abhiman's povI woke up with the most beautiful sight ever.Isha in my arms.

She looked so peaceful to disturb. I planted a kiss on her forehead head and got up from the bed.I did my morning routine and went to my gym.

After 1 hour~

It's raining here And i absolutely hate it . currently it's 7:30 am. I guess Isha must have woken up until now.

I went up only to find Isha dressed up in a beautiful maroon saree. She looks too real to exist.

"Maan ?" She called out. Fvck it. Why does this have to sound so cute?.

"Hukum kariye Maan ki jaan?" I replied adoring her cuteness.

"Hume aapse kuch maangna hai ! Kahiye Hume denge voh cheej Jo hame chahiye?" She asked out.

"Raniya puchti nahi hukum karti hein" i told her folding my hands up to my chest.

"Aap hum-e Rudra se ek l-ast tim-e Mil-ne denge?" At this point my facial features darkened.

"What?" I asked, my voice coming out more deep than i expected.

"Aap hume Rudra se ek l-ast tim-e Milne denge?" She exclaimed more like pleaded this time.

I took few steps closer to her and she started walking backwards until her back came in contact with the wall

"What if I say no?" I said completely caging her in between my arms.

"I know you won't" she said looking straight in my eyes. And i smiled slightly at her confidence.

"You can meet him" i said gently. How could I break the confidence that she was building. If i would have denied today, she would forever hesitate to ask something that she might need.

"Thank youuuuuu" she giggled, and that just made my day better.

PRISHA'S POV

Yesterday I got a text from Rudra. He said he wanted to meet me. And i could not bring myself up to deny it. He deserves an explanation. That is the least I can do.

And I knew Maan, won't reject my appeal.

After bidding my goodbye to Maan, i got ready to meet Rudra.

After 15 mins~

I got ready. The only thing that i needed was to someone drive me to my destination. I know there are more than enough drivers in this palace. But today I wanted someone else to drive me there. The drivers are always busy. Why don't I give them some rest today.

Thinking about this i walked down the stairs.

"Yoo bhabhi-sa!!" Yash said as usual in his cheerful voice.

"Hiii Yash" i greeted him back.

"Going somewhere?" He asked while keeping a small smile over his face.

"Ahh-yes" i said, hesitatingly.

" I am free right now so Want me to drive you there?" He asked as i immediately nodded my head.

"That would be a pleasure" we both laughed and made our way out of the palace.

After 15 mins~

"Here we are" he exclaimed.

"Thanks yash" i gave him my best smile and made my way out of the car.

At the restaurant~

I started waiting for Rudra. He was late as usual.

I saw him walking towards me. I got up from my seat. I looked at him coming towards me.He came near me and gave me a hug. A tight one.

He pulled out of the hug and cupped my face. Surprisingly I didn't feel those butterflies anymore that I used to feel when he used to touch me .

"Let's settle down first" he said and i nodded my head.

"I got to know about this from Abhishek" he said referring to my sudden and unexpected marriage.

"So married and all huh?" He said as soon as we got settled down.

"Yes" i said with a slight smile on my face. I could see how hard he was trying to maintain a smile on his face.

"So how is he? How does he treat you?" He asked, raising his eyebrows.

"He's a gentleman" i replied, honestly.

"I hope you are happy" he said with a slight smile on his face.

"I am more than happy" i replied back genuinely.

"I got to know about your marriage 3 days back when I landed in Delhi. To be honest I was pretty devastated. I cried and all. I asked Abhishek about you and he said you are doing fine with your personal and married life. I could not believe it, that is why I came here to check up on you. Now that I've seen you I can tell you are actually happy with this marriage" he explained.

"You know- I was cut off by him

"If you are going to say "i would never cheat on you or i loved you so much but things weren't in our favour" then please don't. Cause i know you would never do anything like this. I know you loved me." He said, as he smiled, how could he still smile at me. I broke him.

"How do you know that?" I asked, surprised over the fact how he got to know what I was going to say.

"Because i know you" he replied, his eyes welled up with tears.

"Pri?" He called out my name.

"Hmm?" I hummed in response.

"I am leaving India" he said. This is so out of the blue, I did not see that coming.

"Wait- WHAT?" I said digesting what he just stated.

"Yes you heard it right" he said with a slight smile on his face

"I mean w-hy?" I asked him and I don't know why but my eyes got moist

"I have to pri, baccha i don't have any option. Agar mein Aaj ruk gya toh phir shayad kabhi na ja pauga. I have to leave because if I stayed here i would be reminded by the memories we spent together, you sneakingly looking at me. Blushing over my compliments and many more. It will hurt me knowing you are not mine anymore. To be honest I came here prepared, if I saw that you were not happy with this marriage then i would have taken you away with me. But seeing you happy kinda made me happy. I can tell just by looking at that shine of your eyes that you are happy with him. And i wish nothing but you to be happy." He said having warm tears filled up in his eyes

"Rudra can't you stay a lil more" i pleaded

"Sadly I can't. Yes you can call me anytime you want. I am just a call away from you." He said wiping his tears and standing up from his seat.Making me stand up too.

"I'll miss you Rudra" i whispered

"Your husband will kill me if he heard this" he joked trying to lighten up the atmosphere

"So already leaving?" I asked

"Aww is someone going to miss me?" He joked

"Obviously" i said giggling

"Rudra promise me that you'll try to move on from me. And find someone more pretty and kind than me." I said

"I love you pri and nothing can change that, but if i found someone like you then yes that would be an expectation. But the truth is you are a diamond surrounded by stones. And Abhiman was the lucky one to find a rare diamond like you" he replied

"I have to leave now i have a flight within 20 mins. Take care of yourself and yeah if Abhiman troubles you, i am always available." He said winking and giggled. I smacked his arm and gigled with him too.

He engulfed me in a tight hug and bid his final goodbye. And that's how he left. I had tears in my eyes.

I slowly made my way out of the restaurantAnd found it was raining heavily.

As i started walking I slowly got dreanched in the rain.

I walked until I got far away from that restaurant.My phone rang and it displayed "hukum" on screen.

I picked it up.

"Where are you Isha?" He asked

"Somewhere" i said closing my eyes feeling the raindrops falling all over my body.

"What do you mean by that?" He asked impatiently.

"It's raining here! And you are not audible to me" i said.

"Stay wherever you are i am coming there" he said before ending the call.

I got fully drenched in the rain by the time he ended the call

After a 20 mins~

I could see a car coming towards me. And I was well known to it.I could see him rushing towards me.

"Are mad Isha?" He asked.

"I guess" i replied

"Isha you are completely drenched in the rain, how could you even stand here , getting drenched in this rain? I hate it when it rains" he said

Why do you hate the rain so much?" I asked

"Why do you love the rain so much?" He questioned back.

"It makes me feel home." I said. feeling the rain drops falling over her face.

"If someone makes you feel at home means you love them... That means I love you?" He said looking at me as he pulled me closer by grabbing my waist.

Our lips were just an inch away from colliding with one another. At the intensity of his gaze over me i started losing myself into his arms.

"Why didn't you kiss me yet?" I asked yet again losing myself into his deep ocean-like eyes.

"Because when I finally take those lips, melting them into mine, i will let you know that I am yours solely yours , And you will not be merely accepting the fact that you are mine, you will feel what it is like to be mine." With that he crashed his lips onto mine.___________________
_________There first kiss you'll □This one was CUTE Next update on WednesdaySo yeah this is it for today

Chapter 19: Whispers of heart

Author's POV

Their lips met in a lingering kiss, raindrops creating a symphony around them. The world seemed to fade away, leaving only the warmth and passion of their embrace. As the kiss deepened, Prisha felt a whirlwind of emotions, a mix of desire, confusion, and a hint of vulnerability.

Abhimaan's hands moved tenderly, holding her face with a gentle touch. The rain intensified, yet they remained lost in each other. Prisha's mind raced with thoughts – Rudra's departure, her complex feelings, and the undeniable connection she was forming with Abhimaan.

When they finally parted, breathless and drenched, Abhimaan gazed into Prisha's eyes. "Feel that, Isha? That connection?" he whispered, his voice a velvet caress.

She nodded, her heart pounding against her chest. Abhimaan grinned, a playful glint in his eyes.

The rain continued to pour, creating a serene ambiance around them. Abhiman's's concern for prisha warmed her heart.

"Aapko bataun, mujhe barish se nafrat hai," he confessed.

"Kyun?" I questioned, genuinely curious.

"Kyun ki barish mei rehke lagta hai ki kuch kho rahe hein hum, aur kuch paane ko mil nahi raha, par Aaj jab aapko is barish mein bhigta dekha toh humne aapki Kushi payi. Yeh khoobsurat lamha Paya. This rain gave me a memory to cherish. The memory where you let me worship those lips of yours" he explained, his gaze holding a depth that I found intriguing.

And as usual she blushed over his comment

"Now, let's get you home. We wouldn't want you falling sick, would we?"

As they walked back to the car, Prisha couldn't shake off the lingering sensations from the kiss. The confusion in her heart grew, like an unsolved puzzle waiting to be unraveled.

During the drive home, Abhimaan, always the charmer, tried to lighten the mood. "Isha, do you believe in fate?" he asked, his eyes on the road.

She pondered for a moment before answering, "Maybe. Why?"

"Because I think fate brought us together, and in this rain-soaked moment, something changed between us," he replied, a subtle seriousness underlying his words.

Prisha's thoughts swirled as they reached the palace. Yash, Kiara, and Dharya noticed the soaked couple and couldn't resist teasing.

Yash, with a mischievous grin, said, " maa papa dekho who's back? Looks like our Bhaiya and Bhabhi had their own romantic movie scene in the rain!"

Kiara joined in, "I can already see the headlines 'Palace Romance: Abhimaan and prisha's Rainy Affair!'"

Dharya added, "bhai-sa, you're stealing the thunder from every Bollywood hero with such moments."

Abhimaan, taking it all in stride, winked at Prisha, "Well, when she's the leading lady, the script writes itself."

Amidst the laughter, Abhimaan's parents intervened, providing a graceful exit. "Come, let's leave these lovebirds alone. They deserve some peace after being caught in the storm – both literally and figuratively."

As they entered their room, Abhimaan looked at Prisha, a playful glimmer in his eyes. "Ready for the next chapter, Isha?"

She smiled, appreciating the lightness he brought to the situation. Yet, underneath the banter, Prisha couldn't ignore the storm of emotions brewing within her.

That night, as they lay side by side in their room, Abhimaan spoke softly, "Isha, I felt something tonight. Did you?"

Prisha hesitated, uncertainty lingering in her eyes. "I... I don't know, maan. Everything is happening so fast."

He sighed, understanding the turmoil in her heart. . "Sometimes, feelings are complicated, and that's alright. Aapko decide karne ka samay doon ga, par jab tak woh pal nahi aata hai, hum bas yeh pal jeete hain. Aapke andar jo bhi hai, main uska intezaar kar raha hoon. I want you to feel comfortable with me, trust me. And jab tum ready hogi, tab hum apne feelings ko samajh lenge"

With that, they drifted into a contemplative silence. The rain outside continued its rhythmic dance, echoing the unspoken sentiments between them.________________This is it for today □Well i have my exams in January so yeah I will be uploading less frequently.If possible I'll try to upload the next chapter.(if you won't vote i won't upload either)Ohkk so byeee-my Goofballs

Chapter 20: 3.00 am

Prisha's POVI woke up feeling wet down there. Oh holy mother!!! How could I forget my period date !!?!?!???!I rushed inside the washroom. I looked around only to find no pads or tampons available.I used toilet paper to prevent the leaking for a while.I walked out of the washroom.

"Heyyyyyyyyyyyy kanha ji ab hum kya kare!?!?!??!" I asked being frustrated

"Humse mohobbat" i heard a deep voice making me flinch.

Instead of replying i started biting my nails and pacing around the room.

"Bataengi hume kya hua hai ya phir pure mehel ka chakkar lagane ka irada hai?" He asked

"Kuch-

"Phir jhoot?" He asked sternly this time

"Kuch nahi hua hum bol rahe hein na" i said

"Prisha. Don't lie to me I can see clearly through your lies" he said even more sternly this time

"Vo-hume-humare perio-ds chal rahe hein and i don't have any pads at the moment." I said keeping my eyes down on the floor.

"Wait for me I'll get them for you" he said

"It's 3 in the morning I don't think any Shop would be open at this time" i said

"It doesn't matter. All that matters is my wife is in a difficulty and she needs me. And I'll do what i should." He said cupping my cheeks

"I am going out. Wait for me." He said patting my head before leaving

After 40 mins~"Here" he said forwarding a bag towards me, maybe containing pads.

"Thank you" i said

"You don't have to thank me sweetheart. You don't. Instead I am thankful to you that you let me help you." He said

"I will be back in a minute" i said before walking towards the washroom.

As i walked inside the washroom i opened the bag that he brought for me and guess what i saw!?!?!?!??My favourite chocolates, my chiku (incase you forget it's the stuff toy she used to sleep with) and every single brand of pads.

He's so sweet no? I thought before going ahead and changing.

After 10 mins~I got out of the washroom only to find him sitting scrolling over his phone.

"Ahem ahem" I cleared my throat.

"Took you long enough" he said.

I went towards the other side of the bed and laid down There.

"Sleeping already?" He asked.

"Yeah. You should too" i replied in a low volume as my cramps have already started hitting me.

"Is it painful?" He asked and i just hummed.

"Isha come here. Keep your head here" He said taping on his lap. Not having enough energy in me I just obeyed to whatever he said.

He slowly started massaging my scalp, followed by him humming a song. His actions calmed my nerves down. He kept massaging on my scalp until I fall asleep._______________________________Abhiman's POVAs i looked around i couldn't find prisha beside me. I looked over the clock it was 3 in the morning. I saw her coming out of the washroom.

Heyyyyyyyyyyyy kanha ji ab hum kya kare!?!?!??!" She said being frustrated

"Humse mohobbat" i said causing her to flinch.

Instead of replying she started biting her nails and pacing around the room.

"Bataengi hume kya hua hai ya phir pure mehel ka chakkar lagane ka irada hai?" I asked"Kuch-"Phir jhoot?" I asked sternly this time

"Kuch nahi hua hum bol rahe hein na" she said

"Prisha. Don't lie to me I can see clearly through your lies" i said even more sternly this time

"Vo-hume-humare perio-ds chal rahe hein and i don't have any pads at the moment." She said keeping her eyes down on the floor.

"Wait for me I'll get them for you" i said

"It's 3 in the morning I don't think any Shop would be open at this time" she said

"It doesn't matter. All that matters is my wife is in a difficulty and she needs me. And I'll do what i should." I said cupping her cheeks

"I am going out. Wait for me." I said patting her head before leaving.

As i walked out of the palace i hopped onto my bike calling Aadvik and lakshay on the way.

I literally broke every single signal on the way, looking out for a medical store it was too late so unfortunately mostly all the stores were closed.

Finally, i found a medical store open, reaching there I shared my location with Aadvik and lakshay.

After sometime i found Aadvik and lakshay coming towards me, looking sleepy as fuck.

"Bro what the fuck? Why did you call us here? That too in the middle of a sweet night?"

"Shut your mouths and follow me " them being annoyed but still followed me."You both have girlfriends right?" I asked"Did you call us here to discuss this?" Aadvik asked and I shot a glare towards him.

"What type of period pads do girls use?" I asked making them look at me with eyes open wide.

"What the actual Fvck?" They both said at the same time.

"I do not like to repeat myself" i said

"How would we know that?" Aadvik said shrugging his shoulders.

"Idk about pads and stuff but I just know that periods are a actuall bicth and they hurt like fuck. So to Soothe the bicthy pain my girlfriend takes pills, chocolates and ice-cream's and yeah certainly they love to have a teady bear with them" lakshay explained.

"Let's get the pads first" i said walking towards the store, there were plenty of brands there. I got each and every one of those.

"Hume nahi pata tha that the cold and the rude Rajwansh will turn into a "joru ka gulam" after getting married" Aadvik teased

"If being a gentleman and doing the bare minimum concludes in being a "joru ka gulam" then I am more than happy being one" i said walking up to the billing counter

After that I called prisha's brother and asked him to get her stuffed toy.

After being done with all the things i brought the chocolates that I saw her eating with a smile on her face.

After bidding my goodbye with those 2 idiots i hopped onto my bike making my way towards the palace.After 10 mins~

"Here" i said forwarding a bag towards her.

"Thank you" she said.

"You don't have to thank me sweetheart. You don't. Instead I am thankful to you that you let me help you." I replied

"I will be back in a minute" she said before walking towards the washroom.

After 10 mins~"Ahem ahem" she cleared her throat."Took you long enough" i asked to which she didn't reply.

She went towards the other side of the bed and laid down There.

"Sleeping already?" I asked

"Yeah. You should too" she replied in a low volume. And it struck me that Lakshay said that the cramps are a bicth and they HURTS.

"Is it painful?" I asked and she just hummed.

"Isha come here. Keep your head here" i said taping on my lap. And she obeyed I slowly started massaging her scalp, followed by humming a song.

And she fell asleep.I gently laid her head on the pillow and started applying oil on her feets as her feet must be hurting.

After being done with it i washed my hands up and laid beside her. Coconing her in my arms i drifted into a deep slumber.

______________________________This one was CUTE Next update on WednesdaySo yeah this is it for today

Chapter 21 : opening up

On the beautiful occasion of 14k reads A double update____My love for you, like a river, flowsMy heart it swells, as I'm exposedTo your beauty, like a star, aglowYour presence, like a melody, I knowMy love for you, ever trueMy heart, forever, belongs to you.____

____

Abhiman's POVI woke up yet again with the most beautiful sight ever. Isha in my arms.Looking at her peaceful form makes me happy.

I planted a kiss on her forehead and one on either side of her cheeks.Rea ching for my phone i dialled my PA's number.

"Good morning Sir" he said.

"Cancel all my meetings for today" i said coldly.

"Yes Sir" he replied.

I hung up the call.

Getting up from the bed I did some stretching before walking towards the washroom....Being done with my morning routine and gym i looked at the time.

It's 8.30 already.

I walked inside our room, i found prisha sleeping, it's unusual for her to sleep past 8.00 am.

I gently shook her.

She slightly opened her eyes.

"Wake up, jaana" i said gently.

"What's the time?" She asked in a sleepy voice.

"It's 8.30 meri jaan." I replied. Hearing upon this information she woke up with a Jerk but suddenly clutched onto her stomach.

"Ahh" she whimpered.

"Kisne bola tha aapko ese jhatke se uthne ke liye?" I scolded her. Her lips wobbled onto hearing my words.

"Ese roye toh mat ab" i said feeling bad for being the cause of her tears.

"Aap ne hume agar jaldi uthaya hota toh hum late nahi hote" she said with her wobbling lips.

"Aap itni pyari lag Rahi thi sote hue, humara Dil cha ke bhi aapko utha nahi pata" i said but she just turned her face side ways.

"Aapne Hume jaldi kyun nahi uthaya? Hume college ke liye late hogya hei Saab aapki vajah se" she blamed me, she had warm tears flowing from her eyes.

"Haan meri jaan sab humari galti hai, sab humari galti hein, chahe saja de dijiye par ese roye toh mat?" I pleaded feeling vulnerable seeing her tears.

"Chale jaye aap hume nahi baat karni aapse" she said folding her hand over her chest. Oh god her mood swings will kill me !!!!.

"Kaha Jaye hum? Aap hi bta dijiye" i said patiently trying not to get my lil kitty even more angry.

"Somewhere" she replied not looking at me.

"Where will I go huh? You are my home. will someone leave their home? Maybe others will, but definitely not me." I replied back.

"And one more thing you are not going anywhere Isha. Let me take care of you."

"I will go"

"You won't"

"I will"

You won't

"I will"

"Being stubborn are we?" I asked

"I am stubborn and you should have known it before marrying me" she replied

"That I knew . But didn't knew that I was married to a baby " i replied shrugging my shoulder.

"I am just 21 ok you are the oldie here! And yeah you can leave me if you want" she said getting frustrated.

"I won't" i replied

She was about to get up but lost her balance.

She was about to kiss the floor but i caught her midway .

"Sambhal ke chaliya kare meri jaan, is mehel ke raaste aapko kahi bhi gira sakte hein. chahe fir vo kisi ka pyar hi kyun na ho. I said winking at her.

She was about to stand properly but I lifted her up in my arms.

"You should not walk around without wearing any slippers they can cause you cold." I said.

I dropped her infront of the washroom. The washroom had a attached wardrobe in it. Until she's done with her morning routine I'll wait for her.

After 25 mins~

She got out of the washroom in a beautiful red coloured heavy saree. Fuck aur yahan mein pighal gaya!!!!!

"You should dress something comfortable. This saree is looking quite un-comfortable." I said realising that she is on her periods and for all i know someone won't like wearing something this heavy when they are in pain.

"But what about mumma, papaji , chachiji and Chachaji? What if they don't prefer Their daughter in law wearing anything other than Indian- i was cut off by him.

"I don't fucking care about how anyone else prefer you. The only thing that matters is how i prefer you. And I prefer you like the way you prefer being like." I replied. And she just blinked her eyes.

"So now go change your clothes" i said to her and she obeyed my words.

After 6 mins~I saw her coming out of the washroom. Fuck it.She looks like a poison that I am willing to drink.

"Hum kaise lag rahe hain?" She asked

"Bilkul hamari" i replied

"Tha-nk y-ou" she replied. As she was about to walk i immediately lifted her up again.

"I can walk" she said

"And I am fully capable of lifting you" i repliedI walked towards the bed and gently laid her down.

"You won't even lift your finger today ok? I will be the one helping you with everything ok?" She smiled at me and nodded.

"Wait for me I'll get you your breakfast" i saidSaying this i walked downstairs.

"Good morning everyone" i said.

"Good morning beta" dadu and dadi replied back with a gentle smile on their face.

"Meri beti kaha hai?" Maa asked.

"Aapki beti ki tabiyat theek nahi hai" i said.

"Kya hua bhabhi-sa ko?" The three of those idiots asked more like they screamed.

"Kuch nahi hua aapki bhabhi-sa ko just thodi si tabiyat kharab hai" i replied back.

"Maa aap prisha ka khana upar room mein hi bhijwa dijiye" i said and she nodded

Upstairs~

A maid came with a food tray.

"Let's feed you something" i said keeping the food tray on the bed.

"I don't want to eat this" she said with a grumpy face. Isha ke kanha ji bacha lijiye mujhe Isha ke mood swings se!!

"Kya khana chahengi aap?" I asked gently trying to to provoke the "grumpy kid" infront of me

"Ice-cream's and chocolates" she said with a happy face.

"Meri jaan I'll get as many chocolates and ice-creams you want but first you need to eat something healthy ok?" I said cupping her cheeks.

"You'll get me as many as i desire?" She asked.

"Of course meri jaan" i said.

Saying this i started feeding her.

After sometime I was done feeding her

"Now it's time for my chocolates" she said looking like a desperate kid waiting for her candy.

"Let me call my PA he'll bring them within 20 mins" i said about to dial my PA's number on my phone.

"Nahhhhh we'll go and get chocolates and ice-cream's together" she said

"Hamari baat suniye aap, aapki tabiyat theek nahi hai abhi- i was cut off by her.

"Aap hamari baat suniye, aapne kaha tha na haq jtane ko? Lo jata rahe hein hum hamara haq. Aap hamare pati hai and a husband should fulfill his wife's wishes" she said folding her arms over her chest. Oh how I am loving this dominant side of hers.

"Let's go then?" I said with a slight smile on my face.

"YAYYYYY" she screamed

Downstairs~

We reached downstairs only to find my aunt sitting on the sofa.

"Good morning everyone" prisha greeted everyone

"Good morning mera baccha" maa said engulfing her in a warm hug.

"Kaise hai meri bacchi ab?" She asked prisha.

"Theek hain ab hum" she said smiling warmly.

"Sushma meet her. My daughter" maa introduced prisha.

"Is she your daughter in law? Bhabhi ek baat bolugi bura mat manna, meri beti aapki Bahu se laakh darje acchi thi. Look at what she's wearing.How indecent of her to wear this in front of her in-laws-" I cut her off in between

"Biwi hai meri vo or mein kesi Ko ijazat nahi dunga ki koi meri biwi Se is tarah baat kare. She can wear whatever she desires to , And for your kind information if somebody dares to spare a second glance at her then know that her man is Alive and is Fully capable to fight." I said fuming in anger.

"Let's go Isha" i said Interviewing her hands with mine.

Outside~

"You okay meri jaan?" I asked as soon as we stepped out of the palace.

"Don't worry. i am." She said trying her best to smile. The smile that didn't really reach her eyes. I know she's just faking this smile.

"Let's go then?" I said forwarding her my hand and she gladly accepted it.

At the mall~"We are here" i said and went to open the door for her.

"Let's GOOOOOO" she said excitedly and held my hand dragging me with her.

She stopped in front of an ice icecream parlour.

"What would you like to have mam?" One of the waiters asked

"Choco chip, vanilla, chocolate, Butter pecan, Pistachio, Banana split, Rum Raisin and Mint chocolate chip. That's all." She said making my eyes go wide open.

"That's all?" I asked sarcastically. And she nodded while grinning like a kid. Not being the mood spoiler I let her get whatever she wants cause again who am I to snatch that adorable smile off her face ?

"What would you like to have sir?" The waiter asked me.

"A coffee would do" i said

"Will get it within the next 5 mins" the waiter said walking away.

The next 5 mins went with her talking and me listening to her with a smile on my face that i didn't knew existed. Honestly i love this side of hers.The waiter came with our order.

She was the first one to dig in.

"I love this" she said devouring the ice cream. Clearly being in love with the ice-cream's flavour. While I sipped on my coffee.

"Can't you just look at me like the way you look at these ice-creams of yours?" I said clearly jealous of the ice cream.

"Bhukhi nazron se?" She said making me choke on my coffee.

She immediately got up and patted my back.

"Aaram se" she said and got back to her seat.

"Kuch galat bola kya humne?" She asked

"Nahi meri jaan you didn't" why did i even ask her this question. My innocent biwi. I sighed

"Chale ab?" I asked as she was done eating the ice-creams. To which she nodded .

I paid the bill and walked out Interviewning my hands with hers.

I looked at her only to find her staring at a particular store. I looked at what she was looking at.

It was a cosmetic store.

"Isha? I noticed that you don't have much makeup. You can buy them if you want." I said.

"Can I?" She asked.

"Ofcourse you can meri jaan. You don't have to ask me." I said

We walked inside the store and she stopped infront of a shelf containing lipsticks in it.She started checking them all out. But couldn't get the write shade. As she was overviewing them.

"You should try them on" i said

"We can't try it on our lips" she replied

"Wait i have an idea" she said with a glint of mischief in her eyes.

"Spill the beans already" i said.

"Can I try them on your hands?" She asked with puppy eyes. And as usual i gave in.

She tried them on the back of my hands. After finding something similar to her taste she selected it.

Paying the bill we walked out of the store.We had our dinner outside today.

The best thing about today was her opening up to me

heading out of the mall we got into the car and went straight towards the palace. It was already late.

Prisha has already slept. I carried her up the room and tucked her inside the warm comforter. Changing onto something comfortable i too joined her.

And before i knew i fell asleep with her in my arms.______________________
____

Ignore the typos i wrote this one in a hurry Btw This one was CUTE Next update on Friday So yeah this is it for today

Chapter 22: haunting past

Prisha's POVIt's already 9pm.Sitting onto the bed I was lost in my thoughts.

This week was just like an adventure.It was a weekend full of care and love given by Abhiman.The way he handled all my mood swings and cravings kinda melted me.Thinking about all this my phone rang and it was Abhishek.I picked it up.

"Hieeeeeeeeeeeeeeee" i said cheerfully.

"Mein yaad bhi hun ya bhul gayi ?" He asked.

"Ummm, tu vahi hein na? Jiski bandar jaise shakal hai?" I giggled saying this.

"Ane de mujhe udhar mein btata hun tujhe" he warned but later giggled.

"Aur bta? Sab theek?" I inquired.

"Haan sab badhiya. Tu bta apni love life ke bare mein" he teased.

"Dhat pagle, kuch bhi bolta hai" i tried changing the topic.

"Acha bta... acha hai na vo? Tu khush toh hai na pri?" He asked making my heart swelled up with warmth.

"Arey Han baba, mein khush hun. Bohot khush" i replied honestly.

"Kal ka kya plan hai?" He asked making me confused.

"Kal ka? Kal kya hai?" I asked being confused.

"Tera birthday hai meri maa. Bhul gayi?" He said.

"Tujhe pta hai na Abhi? I don't like celebrating my birthday?" I said more like mumbled.

"Pri? Why are you relating it to your birthday huh?" He asked.

"Because it was related to it" i replied.

"Pri meri baat sun! would your parents and your brother like it if you don't celebrate your special day?" He gently said

"I want no arguments on this" i told him this trying to dismiss this argument.

"And I will argue on it" he replied back stubbornly.

"You know me too well, and you know that I do not like celebrating my birthdays" i said in a low volume it was merely a whisper. I was on the verge of breaking down.

"But- I cut him off in between.

"Please Abhi" i pleaded choking onto my tears.

"Ro toh mat, theek hai! I won't force you please stop crying naa?" He pleaded.

"I-i w-ill ca-ll yo-u in a bi-t" i said hanging up the call.

After 15 mins, I took a deep breath in and out, and wiped my tears off.

I sighed walking towards the balcony.I sat there on the swing.

I looked up to the sky, "i love you mumma papa and bhaiya" i said with my eyes dripping with tears.

I cried for a good time and eventually fell asleep on the swing itself.____
_______________________________Abhiman's POV

I came into the room straight from work.I looked around the room but couldn't find Isha anywhere. I further searched for her in the washroom. But it was of no use.

I could feel a fear gripping in my heart. The sweat beads on my forehead were telling about my anxiousness, the anxiousness i never felt. The anxiousness of losing someone that I felt years ago. I am feeling it again. But this is something different. It's about her. My wife. My love. My Isha.

I looked around to find that the balcony was open.

Going there i saw prisha sleeping on the swing.

I took a breath of relief.

I went close to her. I sat on my knees admiring her. I caressed her cheeks only to find them wet. My eyes travelled over her eyes. I touched her lashes to find tears stuck in them.

I could hear and feel something. A voice. A voice of my shattering heart. A feeling of rage. Rage for the reason behind her tears.

A wave of cold wind splashed over us, making her shiver slightly. As she was wearing an alluring saree, her waist was uncovered making her feel cold.

I snaked my arms over her waist only to feel something on her back. Something like a scar maybe? Before i could think anything she shivered over my mere touch and opened her eyes as fastly as she could. She seemed frightened.She immediately pushed me away and sat straight up.

"Do not come close to me" she said curling up in a ball, with a glint of fear in her hazel brown eyes. Is she scared because I touched her?

"Stay away from me pankaj, stay away, please, i beg you." She Shivered as she said those words. Pankaj? Who's he? Whoever he might be, he surely is a part of her past. A bad past.

"I am Maan. Your Maan." I said as she seemed to mistook me as that fucker.

"Maan?" She asked whispering as if confirming it. I slowly with slow steady steps went in her direction keeling in front of her. As she looked into my eyes. I took her hands in mine gently.

"Your Maan" i confirmed, and the tears that were halted in those hazel brown eyes for the past one minute started flowing.

I got on her level and gently embraced her in my arms, As she melted in the warmth of my arms.

"I a-m tir-ed of b-eing stro-ng Maan" she told me , hiccuping.

"I know meri jaan. And you should know that you are allowed to be weak in front of me." I said gently caressing her hair, as she hid her face in the Crook of my neck.

"He w-as t-here ag-ain." She exclaimed looking frightened.

"Who's he?" I asked as my eyes darkened at the mention of that particular "he".

"Monster" she said trembling as she mentioned that word.

"Maan h-e'll ta-ke me aw-ay ag-ain. I d-on't w-ant to lea-ve yo-u. I don't li-ke him" she said and i could sense the storm inside her.

"Meri jaan, no one. I repeat NO ONE can take something that is mine ok? You are mine aren't you?" I asked her.

"Yes. I am yo-urs." She managed to talk between her hiccups.

"That's like my wife" i said. And she lifted her head up from my shoulder she looked at me with those red blooded eyes of hers. I swear to her I will drown that fucker in the color of her eyes, that will be nothing but his own blood.

"Meri jaan do you want to share something, hmmm?" I asked. And she nodded her head in no, with those wobbling lips of hers.

"Can I know why you don't want to share it?" I asked cause I wanted to know whether she was hesitant to share it or not comfortable sharing it with me.

"I have nothing to share" she said with her eyes hung low. So she's hesitant. i lifted her chin up with my index finger.

"I want to listen to it either it's something or absolutely nothing. I am here to listen all of it." I replied with a small smile.And a lone tear escaped from her eyes, before it could slide down her cheeks i kissed it.

"I was 3 and it was my birthday so me , my parents and my brother decided to celebrate it. We booked a restaurant and were on the way to it and everything changed in a span of seconds. We met an accident unfortunately I was the only one who survived. I was alone and none of my relatives cared to take me with them. At the end I was sent to foster care. And that was where baba used to go to give charity and one day he saw me and got fond of me. He visited me in regular intervals. And one day he came with bhaiya and di and they were there to adopt me. I was so happy that day but it didn't last long. As we all reached home I got to know that baba adopted me without maa's knowledge. That day maa was so, angry that she told baba to leave me over the streets but baba somehow managed to convince her.

That day was the first time i felt bad for existing. And from that day maa is angry at me. She doesn't love me. But baba, bhaiya and di loves me." She said with tears flowing from her eyes but still a smile was on her lips, maybe a smile of loneliness. But the question arises: were her adoptive parents the reason behind the nightmares that she gets? Did they abuse her?

"Isha? Did they perhaps abuse you? Verbally? Physically? Mentally? Did they?" I asked as my eyes darkened over the fact someone was hurting her.

"Noooooooo, they didn't" she said immediately.

"Isha if you are comfortable, can i ask you something?" I asked.

"Hmm" she hummed. Getting the permit i asked.

"What is the reason behind your nightmares?" I asked taking her soft hands into mine. Hearing upon me her head rose up immediately. And the tears that seemed to stop made their way again out of her eyes.

"Maan you will leave me after knowing the truth" she spoke those words out making me wonder..did i fail making her realise how insanely, madly, deeply, selflessly i am in love with her? now even if she herself asks me to leave her, i won't.

"I do not leave things that are mine. You were, you are and you will be forever inked in the color of my love." I replied kissing her eyes.

"I won't force you to share it. Only if you are comfortable" i cleared her. She should know that nothing is more important to me more than her.

"I was in 10th an-d there was a guy, he-he propose-d to me in fro-nt of the whole sch-ool, and at that time i wasn't ready for any rel-ationship and moreo-ver he looked quite old. And I did what see-med right to me at th-at tim-e. I politely rejec-ted him. And th-at was the biggest mistake of my life. The following day-s i f-elt someon-e stalkin-g me. I felt tha-t someo-ne was obse-rving my each and ever-y move. I igno-red it think-ing that i mu-st be overth-inking it. And th-at was the se-cond bi-ggest mistake i made. The n-ext day i ha-d ex-tra classes and it was around 6.30 pm a-nd I was alo-ne, Abhis-hek was ab-sent that- day. A-nd the al-ey that I was wa-lking on w-as darker than usual. And th-at was when I heard foot-steps behind me. I was fast enough to kno-w that som-eone was followi-ng me. I starte-d run-ning And t-he person wh-o was follow-ing me star-ted run-ning behi-nd me. Su-ddenly i felt an ir-on rod over my he-a-d and the onl-y thin-g t-hat i re-member befo-re blacki-ng ou-t was. "IT'S THE END OF HIDE AND SEEK SWEETY".I -woke up to an unk-nown pla-ce. I tri-ed m-oving on-ly to find- out i was tied- on a ch-air with ropes. I stru-ggled but it was of abs-olute no use. O-ne thi-ng w-as clea-r th-at we are in an apart-ment cl-ose to a roa- d ma-ybe bec-ause i co-uld h-ear the tra-ffic ver-y clea-rly I wa-s trying to o-pen the ropes whic-h i was tied to. And there came a crac-king voice at the door. And i f-ound the guy who proposed to me. A fe-ar grip-ped ov-er my heart. The e-vil smile of h-is was cree-ping me out. The swea-t bea-ds appe-ared ov-er my forehe-ad. He cam-e towa-rds m-e and sta-rted tracin-g my fa-ce with his ind-ex finger despite my plead-ings. I was scar-ed of what he mig-ht do next. I was disg-usted by his touch-es. His finger slowly lo-w over my cleav-age. I screa-med and beg-ged b-ut he tore my-my-my sleeves. I co-uld feel m-y soul getti-ng staine-d wit-h his dirt-y touche-s ov-er my bod-y. The thi-ng he said next was eno-ugh to make me numb. He came cl-ose to my ear-s and whisp-ered "we are getting married tom-orrow Sweety, and don't worry I am a gentleman ok? Don't be scared of me." It creep-ed me out in a way nothing else cou-ld. I was so scared Maan. I was so sca-red. He disgus-ted me. I w-as disgust-ed with my body. I wa-s disgus-ted with his touch-es. It w-as 6 in the m-orning i co-uld tell because the-re was a clo-ck hun-g o-n t-he w-all . I was silen-tly weeping while that ma-niac was asl-eep. And then some-thing strick over my bra-in. I had bang-les on my wr-ists. And so-me of it was bro-ken by no-w. I slow-ly started trying cuttin-g the ropes with the bro-ken bangl-es over my wri-sts by rub-bing them against the ro-pe. And to my lu-ck I was succes-sful. I ever so slo-wly got up fro-m the chair. Bu-t the pr-oblem was he was sleepi-ng just in fro-nt of me o-n the couch. I slow-ly slow-ly start-ed ma-king my wa-y tow-ards the doo-r. I was ab-out 5 steps away fro-m the do-or and tha-t mon-ster's s-leep got brok-en becau-se i accidentally hit the flo-wer va-s. And i looked behi-nd only to fin-d h-im gettin-g up. I could n-ot t-hink of anyt-hing other tha-n runni-ng away and I di-d. I opene-d the d-oor and was about to step ou-t he pul-led -me by the he-m of m-y ku-rti wit-h s-uch an-d inten-sity th-at i-t to-re away and pul-led me towa-rds hi-m w-ith a Jer-k an-d stabbe-d mult-iple tim-es ov-er m-y b-ack mak-ing m-e screa-m lou-der tha-n i eve-r d-id. A-nd la-ter he p-ulled ou-t a gu-n and sh-ot m-e And ag-ain bef-ore blacking out i heard him sayi-ng"AGAR PRISHA PANKAJ KI NAHI TOH KISI AUR KI BHI NAHI"And i blac-ked out. Whe-n i woke u-p i foun-d tha-t I w-as in a hosp-ital surroun-ded by ba-ba bha-iya and di. They to-ld me th-at i blacke-d out an-d the-re were peop-le aroun-d that ar-ea, hear-ing me shout they rescu-ed me. And wh-en I as-ked them about that guy they just said that he was in a plac-e he deserv-es to b-e." She said hiccuping badly i gently took her onto my lap and she cried more and more over my shoulder. ("I was in 10th and there was a guy, he-he proposed to me in front of the whole school, and at that time i wasn't ready for any relationship. And I did what seemed right to me at that time. I politely rejected him. And that was the biggest mistake of my life. The following days i felt someone stalking me. I felt that someone was observing my each and every move. I ignored it thinking that i must be overthinking it. And that was the second biggest mistake i made. The next day i had extra classes and it was around 6.30 pm and I was alone, Abhishek was absent that day. And the aley that I was walking on was darker than usual. And that was when I heard footsteps behind me. I was fast enough to know that someone was following me. I started running And the person who was following me started running behind me. Suddenly i felt an iron rod over my head and the only thing that i remember before blacking out was. "IT'S THE END OF HIDE AND SEEK SWEETY".I woke up to an unknown place. I tried moving only to find out i was tied on a chair with ropes. I struggled but it was of absolute no use. One thing was clear that we are in an apartment close to a road maybe because i could hear the traffic very clearly. I was trying to open the ropes which i was tied to. And there came a cracking voice at the door. And i found the guy who proposed to me. A fear gripped over my heart. The evil smile of his was creeping me out. The sweat beads appeared over my forehead. He came towards me and started tracing my face with his index finger despite my pleadings. I was scared of what he might do next. I was disgusted by his touches. His finger slowly hung low over my cleavage. I screamed and begged but he tore my-my-my sleeves. I could feel my soul getting stained with his dirty touches over my body. The thing he said next was enough to make me numb. He came close to my ears and whispered "we are getting married tomorrow Sweety, and don't worry I am a gentleman ok? Don't be scared of me." It creeped me out in a way nothing else could. I was so scared Maan. I was so scared. He disgusted me. I was disgusted with my body. I was disgusted with his touches. It was 6 in the morning i could tell because there was a clock hung on the wall . I was silently weeping while that maniac was asleep. And then something strick over my brain. I had bangles on my wrists. And some of it was broken by now. I slowly started trying cutting the ropes with the broken bangles over my wrists by rubbing them against the rope. And to my luck I was successful. I ever so slowly got up from the chair. But the problem was he was sleeping just in front of me on the couch. I slowly slowly started making my way towards the door. I was about 5 steps away from the door and that monster's sleep got broken because i accidentally hit a flower vas making it fall, And i looked behind only to find him getting up. I could not think of anything other than running away and I did. I opened the door and was about to step out he pulled me by the hem of my kurti with such and intensity that it tore away and pulled me towards him with a Jerk and stabbed multiple times over my back making me scream louder than i ever did. And later he pulled out a gun and shot me. And again before blacking out i heard him saying"AGAR PRISHA PANKAJ KI NAHI TOH KISI

AUR KI BHI NAHI"And i blacked out. When i woke up i found that I was in a hospital surrounded by baba bhaiya and di. They told me that i blacked out and there were people around that area, hearing me shout they rescued me. And when I asked them about that guy they just said that he was in a place he deserves to be.")

"Don't worry Mera baccha. You are a beautiful rose adored with painful thrones that is your past now. You showed me your thrones and now it's my duty to show you your man, man that is willingly going to bleed by your thrones if you asked him to" I said As i gently caressed her back. I kept Caressing her back until i could hear her breathing get slow and steady. I took that as a sign and lifted her up in my arms yet again i could feel her scar. And the anger intensified that was bubbling inside me. I was calm. Only because she was there beside me. If I had gotten to know this before I don't know what i would have done.

I gently laid her down on the bed.

I knew what exactly i had to do....________________As promised the chapter is HEREEEEEEEEE Don't forget to vote This is it for today Hope you liked it.(ignore the typos)Don't forget to drop a commentI saw the comments on the last chapter you guys are soooooooooooo cute □I love you all so muchMah goofballs □Next update would be on the upcoming week (Saturday) □Ohk then bye-e goofballs

Chapter 23: birthday

Guys it's finally her birthday (it's my birthday too hehe □)Hope you enjoy reading itHappy reading

---

Abhiman's POV

I knew exactly what I had to do now.The feelings that I am feeling right now will either have me taking the life of that fucker or will lead me to kill myself for not being there when she needed me. Needed me to heal her. Love her. Care for her. I was not there.

I dialled a number of the DSP.

"Good evening sir" he greeted.

"I want all the information about the case 4 years back registered in the name of prisha singhania" i ordered.

"On the work sir. Will inform you in an hour" he informed.

"30 mins. I want it in 30 mins" I stated in my cold voice. I hung up the call before he could respond.I looked at her sleeping form. She looked like something i would never get tired of.

I walked closer to her and removed a strand of hair falling over and covering her beautifully sculpted face.

"Bohot badi bhakt hai ye aapki Isha ke kanha ji. Aap bas aapki is bhakt ko khush rakhna. Kuch manga nahi hai aapse kabhi, aaj maangta hu mein meri biwi, meri mohabbat, meri Isha ki khushi." I said Caressing her jaw.

I looked at the clock that was just 5 mins away from stricking 12.

It is her birthday tomorrow.

The birthday of my heart beat, my soul, the soul that has me wrapped up into a mess. A mess that only can be solved by her.

I heard a knock over the door, confused about who it was at this late at night I went to open it.

Only to find the 3 idiotic creatures aka my siblings dressed up looking like a joker, with a clown nose, party propers and a cake in Kiara's hand.

"Bhabi-sa so Rahi hein?" Yash being the dumb one asked.

"Nahi toh, ghoomar kar rahi hein. Dekhna chahoge?" I said with sarcasm dripping from my tongue.

Dharya hit his arms and turned to face me."We just wanted to be the first one to wish bhabi-sa" he said with puppy eyes followed by the other 2 clown looking creatures looking at me with their puppy eyes.

"And you think I am going to let that happen? I will be the one to wish her first" i said smiling evily.

"You can't do that" Kiara argued.

"I can" i debated back.

"You can't"

"I can"

"You can't"

"I-" i was cut off in between by Maa.

"stop it you both" said maa popping out of nowhere followed by dad, chachu , Chachi dadi and dadu.

"I will be the one wishing my child first" maa said dismissing Kiara's and my debate.

"But-

"No arguments i said" she ordered making Kiara's and my face fall.

"All preparations done?" I asked and all of them nodded their heads in yes.

"Guys 10 seconds are left" dharya announced.All of us tiptoed and went towards prisha.

"3. 2. 1" We counted.

"HAPPY BIRTHDAY PRIIIIIIIIIIIIIIIIIIIII" we shouted making her open her eyes wide.

She looked up and sat straight.

"Happy Birthday meri laado" maa wished keeping a hand over her head.

"Happy Birthday beta" papa said smiling

"Happy Birthday baccha" Chachi and chacha wished

"Happy Birthday gudiya" dadu wished

"Happy Birthday meri bacchi" wished dadi .

"HAPPY BIRTHDAY TO THE BEST BHABHI-SA IN THE WORLD"
Kiara, dharya and Yash screamed.Isha had a river flowing from her eyes.

"Than-k-you s-o m-uch" she said while having water filled up in her eyes

Kiara siglaned me to take her where we had planned the surprise.

"Isha meri jaan close your eyes" i said and she looked confused but still gave
in to my demand. I kept my palms over her eyes

I slowly yet carefully held her forearms to help her get up. I gently led her to
the terrace, followed by others.Reaching upon there i removed my palms.
Seeing the decor a low gasp left her mouth.

She turned around to find everyone making a heart with their hands.

"Thank youuuuuu soooooooooooooooooooooooooooo muchhhhhhh-
hhhhhhhhhhhhhhhhhh all of you" she cried in happiness. I kneeled in front
of her.

"Arey meri jaan bas bhi Karo ab. I hate it when you cry because it urges me
to kiss you. And i cannot kiss you in front of everyone Or can I?" I teased
her and kissed her tears away, making her covered with all red shades of
hues.

"Ohhhhhhhhhhhhhhhhhhhhhhhhooooooooooooooooo" everyone present in
their teased.She hid her face in my arms.

"Ohk so cut this cake real quick bhabhi-sa" Kiara said breaking our not-so
romantic moment. She said and brought the cake on the bed.

She handed Isha a knife.

Instead of cutting the cake she looked upon maa.

"Kya hua laadoo?" Maa asked going closer to her.

"Mumma can you lend me your hand? I want to cut this cake with you and papa" she said with some warm water in her eyes.

"Hayeeeeee meri bacchi" maa said as she sits beside her followed by dad.

They cut the cake together while we sang her a birthday song.

As she took a piece of cake in her hand maa and papa was the first one to have it, followed by us.Having the cake and giving Isha some warm hugs they wished her for the last time before retiring to their rooms.

In the meantime I lifted her up in my arms while she stared at me.

Closing the door i kept her down, as i faced her.

"Happy birthday Rani saheba, Everyone else can have their 13.8 billion-year-old universe. While I'd love to have my universe. My 22-year-old universe" i wished kneeling down, as i revealed a flower bouquet containing 520 exact flowers in it. It's said that, 520 is an acronym for "i love you"

"Than-k y-ou" she shuttered as she took the bouquet off of my hands she lowered her eyes due to her shy and timid self.

" For the next 24 hours I am nothing more than your humble servant. (just like how I'd be for the other 364 days). I said and whispered the last sentence huskily into her ears.She looked up for a second and again laid her eyes on the floor.

"Isha you know what? I feel jealous. Jealous of that fucking floor because I want you to have your eyes on me only on me, but whenever I am around you love to gaze at this lovely floor of yours"

"Humari in masoom si Aankon ko bus aapki hi talash rehti hei, aap bhi to humse nazre milaya kariye, kya aapki nazron ko meri nazron ki talash nahi hoti?" i stated in a poetic way trying to impress her but instead of saying anything she laughed wholeheartedly.

SHE LAUGHED. FOR THE FIRST TIME IN FRONT OF ME.

"Didn't expect you to be so poetic" she said giggling.

"When you are the actor, the script writes itself" i said winking at her making her laugh her heart out.

"you just made my day" i said smiling like a fool.

"How?" She asked still wearing that beautiful smile.

"By making that sweet sound. The sound i would love to hear my life long. The sound i would choose over any music." I said as i lifted her up making her relieve a slight scream.

"How can you lift me like i weigh nothing? Ain't i am heavy?" She asked. Who gave her the right to say that she's heavy? She's literally a 22 year old trapped in the small body of a 5 year old.

"You will never be heavy for me meri jaan. In my embrace, your weight becomes a feather, effortlessly wanting to be carried by the strength of my love for you." i said as she kept her head over my chest.

"Your heart Beats are so fast " she whispered closing her eyes.

"Kuch aawazen khas hoti hai, aur aap vo awwaz hein hamari. I am a love-struck symphony, and you're the blushing note that makes my heart sing. i said and she hummed as she was on the verge of falling asleep. She snuggled more into me. I could bet if she was in her senses right now she would have been a blushy mess.

The thing that i noticed is that she is a very light sleeper. If I put her down right now she will wake up.

What should I do? I can't afford to snatch this peaceful look off her face , can I ? ABSOLUTELY NOT.

I will carry her in my arms until she gets some deep sleep.I started humming a low tune to help her sleep, while strolling around the room.

After 32 mins~

I could hear her low baby-like , muffled snores. And what could be a better sign than that of falling asleep?

I gently laid her down on the bed. I covered her up with the comforter and myself too.

And eventually fell asleep with her in my arms, forgetting about that fucker's information.___________________________Ohk so first of all we are 30k □ and I am soooooooooooooooooooooooooooooo muchhhhhhhhhhhhhhhhhhhhhhhhhhh thankful to all of you Second thing despite being 30k the votes are still around one thousand.I am putting my soul in this book and the only thing that I want from you guys is to vote for it.And I am serious on this if you guys won't vote i won't upload either (Sorry for being rude Ilyasm □)And yeah one of the goofballs commented and asked if the shayri's that i write in beginning of the chapters. YES i write them myself, but there's some lyrics taken from some songs ♡

Vote target 100

ANNOUNCEMENT

Hieeeeeeeeeeeeeee myyyyyyyyyyyyy goofballsssssssss! Your author here!

I just wanted to say that thank youuuuuu sooooooooooooooooooooooooooo muchhhhhhhhhhhhhhhhhhhhhhhh-hhh for 45k+ views on this book□

Bhai i am literally burning up right now□I was good until yesterday, i was writing a new chapter but considering that it was late now i decided to sleep and laid down and in half an hour I was like burning at 102 degrees. My eyes were burning hot and I was literally crying. But I am kinda fine now! Pray for me goofballs □

And about updates well, my uploading isn't scheduled. But just for you guys I will be uploading every Saturday□(Because That is the only day i get for myself!) Hope you don't mind!

Once again thank youuuuuu sooo much for 45k+ viewsAnd guys you all are so cute! I read almost every single comment and it makes me happy ! Thank you !

Take care!I love you all□!Your author~

Chapter 24: The whole day

Heyyyyyyyyyy goofballs!We have officially completed 3k votesssssssss!!!! (An early update for you'all)

Thank youuuuuu sooooooooooooooooooooooooooo muchhhhhhhhhhhhhhhhhhhhhhhhhhhh you'all

And yeah your get well soon comments made me feel sooooo good □□

(READ THIS BEFORE CONTINUING)

I am literally so happy about that...but...I encountered a hate comment yesterday. And i blocked that person. That person wrote so many bad things because i didn't pair prisha with rudra. Does that even make sense? I have already said in the introduction part that this is a love triangle and if you are sensitive don't continue this story! I was literally burning sick yesterday! And this sort of behaviour won't be accepted! I know I am being kind of rude but goofballs I can't help it....you know i have been trying to manage both my book and personal stuff and if you guys will behave like this then of course it will make me feel demotivated. Please let me know your thoughts in the comment section!

~your author ___________________________________Sorry for being rude but that wasn't for you my lil goofballs, it was for some idiotic creatures

And yeah one of the lil goofballs asked me in my DM if there's any explicit scene in this book. Sorry to say but this is an old schooled romance book / closed door romance. Hope you'all won't mind ♡___________________________________Ishare aankhe karti gyiLab unhe dhakte gye~Ain___________________________________

Author's POV

Prisha awoke to the soft glow of morning light, her room adorned with twenty elegantly wrapped gifts. She looked around but couldn't find Abhiman. She got up and rubbed her eyes to clear her vision. As she got She looked around in search of her phone but instead she felt hands snaking around her waist.

"Happy birthday, meri jaan" Abhiman whispered, his eyes filled with affection. Prisha felt a warmth in her heart.

"Thank you" she said facing him.

"My pleasure darling" he said as he bowed dramatically making her giggle.

After their little romantic moment prisha walked into the washroom to complete her morning business.

As she walks in her sight held a view of a bouquet filled with roses and a chit over it.

The chit said "ye phool mere phool ke liye ♡" the chit was adorned with a lil cute heart at the end.With a constant smile over her face she walked out of the washroom with a cute dress that she found hanging in the bathroom with a chit attached that said "the dress will be honoured if you cared you wear it". She giggled recalling that chit.

"Jaan lene ka irada hai kya mohtarma?" Abhiman playfully Said as soon as his sight fell on his beloved wife.

"Humara jaan lene ka toh nahi par aapka Dena ka irada lagta hai" she played along making his eyes go wide as this was something he never expected. But he felt content that she finally was opening up to him.

"Sahi lagta hai aapko" and their come his old Isha back again blushing over his ways around words.

After their cute romantic moment they decided to walk down the dining hall and greet everybody.

"Good morning Mumma" said prisha in her loud melodious and chirpy voice.

"Good morning meri laado" Abhiman's mother reciprocated the enthusiasm.

"Aaj meine meri laado ke liye sab kuch uski pasand ka bnaya hai" she said lovingly placing her hand over prisha's head.

"Bhabi-sa this is for you" said Kiara kneeling down with a rose in her hand.

"Awwwwww" prisha couldn't help but gaze at the rose being awestruck. She accepted the rose and hugged Kiara

"Bhabi-sa dekhiye humne aapke liye aapki favourite chocolates layi hein" said dharya while forwarding a box of Ferrero rocher. Making her feel all giddy. And with an instant she hugged both Kiara and dharya. While Abhiman stood there adoring her bond that she had formed with his siblings.

"It's not fair guys, bhabi-sa aap hume kaise bhul sakti hein!!" came a whining voice of a very dramatic Yash.

"Join us" i said giggling and he ran up to us and we did a group hug.

"Enough now. Let my wife take a breath you guys are literally squeezing the life out of her" said Abhiman walking towards them and freeing prisha from their hold.

They ate their breakfast in peace, while Talking, giggling and teasing each other.

~~~~~~

As the morning unfolded, Abhiman continued to surprise her with gifts every hour. From a stunning dress that he insisted she wear for the evening to a rare book signed by her favorite author, the day became a symphony of affectionate gestures. Abhiman has planned to give her exactly 22 gifts as she has turned 22 today.

~~~~~~~

By the time the clock struck 3 pm,

Kiara came to her room and called her downstairs.Reaching upon there she saw Abhimaan with a guitar and all the family members around there. The room was beautifully decorated with her pictures.

As soon as she stepped there he started playing, while singing along with the rhythm it..

Dekheya main chand dekheyaNooran wale sitare dekheyaPar tere jaisa na koi dekheya main

He was looking deep into her song while singing it making her flustered.

Lagta hai nigahon mein teriBin doobe rehna hi nahiMujhe ishq yeh karne seAb koi bhi na rok sakeya..

He handed the guitar to dharya, and got up from his seat, while dharya continued playing the guitar. Abhimaan didn't stop singing the song yet started stepping towards prisha...he forwarded his hand and she took it into hers. He held her close, one hand on her waist, while she placed her hand gently on his shoulder. They moved together in sync with the music, creating a simple yet intimate dance that spoke of familiarity and connection.

O haareya main dil haareyaO haareya main dil haareyaO haareya main dil haareyaMain haara tujhpe o..

O hareya main dil hareyaO hareya main dil hareyaO hareya main dil hareyaMain haara tujhpeMain haara tujhpe o..

Abhiman continued to sing the song and Their movements were effortless, a natural flow of steps that reflected a comfort born from shared moments on and off the floor. The subtle pressure of his hand on her waist guided her steps, and her hand on his shoulder communicated a silent assurance. As they navigated the floor, the world around them blurred, leaving only the two of them immersed in the rhythm of the music and the unspoken language of their dance. In those moments, the ordinary became extraordinary, and the dance floor transformed into a space where the language of touch and movement conveyed a story of closeness and understanding.

As their dance ended everyone hooted for them making prisha hide her face in Abhiman's embrace.

~~~~~~

The clock struck at 4 pm.

"Isha? Wanna go out?" Abhiman asked looking at prisha with a slight smile on his face."Sure" prisha replied and reciprocated the smile but this was much bigger than that of Abhiman.
~~~~~~

As they both walked out of the palace hand in hand providing each other with warmth. They hopped onto his bike and left for the restaurant. As they reached there Abhiman took her on the rooftop . They were on the rooftop, as Abhiman looked at prisha like she was the only available yet the beautiful scenery to look around.

"To twenty two years of your beautiful existence and the joy you bring to my life," Abhiman toasted, his gaze locked onto hers. Prisha felt a flutter in her chest, the gravity of his words settling into her soul.

~~~~~~~~

The clock strucked 6pm.

"Let's eat" Abhiman said, remembering that the only proper meal prisha ate was her breakfast.

"As you wish" prisha replied as she herself felt hungry.

~~~~Post-dinner, they wandered through the city streets, hand in hand. The world seemed to fade away as they shared dreams, aspirations, and the magic of being around each other. Abhiman's eyes held a secret, a sentiment waiting to be unveiled.

As the clock approached 7 pm, prisha found herself gifted with a bouquet of twenty rare flowers. Each bloom held a silent promise, and Abhiman's eyes betrayed emotions he hadn't spoken aloud.

"Isha, these flowers symbolize the beauty you've brought into my life ." he confessed, his voice tender.

After that they went shopping~

Abhiman brought prisha a stunning gown.

The anticipation grew, a quiet understanding that the grand finale awaited at the stroke of midnight.

"Isha? Can you wear this dress for me?" Abhiman said. Making her agree.

"Sure" prisha said and went to the changing room.

The clock struck at 8 pm, and prisha found herself slipping into the stunning dress Abhiman had gifted her earlier. It draped elegantly around her, the embodiment of his impeccable taste. As they stood before the mirror, Abhiman's eyes reflected a mixture of admiration and a hint of vulnerability.

"You're breathtaking, prisha" he uttered, his voice carrying a sincerity that left her momentarily breathless.

The evening unfolded with grace and extravagance. They ate ice-cream in a private alcove, the soft glow of candlelight casting a warm ambiance.

They talked, laughed, giggled, and enjoyed each other's company.

As the clock neared 9 pm, prisha found herself immersed in the enchantment of the evening. The anticipation now palpable, Abhiman guided her toward a waiting limousine.

"Where are we heading to?" Prisha asked with confusion visible on her face

"Our next destination awaits," he declared with a mischievous glint in his eyes.

The limousine meandered through the city, eventually stopping at a fair that seemed to materialize from a dream. The air was filled with the scent of cotton candy and the sounds of soft music playing in the background. A carousel, adorned with twinkling lights, beckoned them.

"I wanted tonight to be a kaleidoscope of memories, prisha," Abhiman admitted, his hand finding hers. They strolled through the fair, indulging in sweet treats and relishing the simple pleasures of shared amusement.

"Suniye!" Prisha said tugging onto the sleeves of abhiman's blazer.

"Sunaiye?" Abhiman said melting at the way she called him.

"Hume voh stuff toy chahiye" said prisha pointing at a cute toy.

"Kya karenge aap uska? Hum hein na" Abhiman said teasing her but she didn't look convinced.

"Please?" He already did melt at her cute plea but decided to tease her a Lil.

"Aap hamari male sautan laa Rahi hein?" He asked making a cute pout. Making her giggle at his cute face. After the little act of his , he bought her the stuff toy.

The wandered hand in hand exploring the fair.

~~~~~

As the clock approached 11 pm, they found themselves under a sky bursting with fireworks. Abhiman's eyes held a secret, a revelation reserved for the stroke of midnight.

"The moon looks pretty right?" Prisha said looking up at the sky.

"Jo bolta hai vahi hota hai" Abhiman playfully replied while smirking,making her cover with the red hues.

"Aapko pata hai? Hume Chand bohottt pasand hai" she said gazing at the moon.
~~~~~

"Itna self-obsessed hona accha nahi hota" he said and at first she looked confused but then it sturk that he was calling her a moon. Realising she widened her eyes making him giggle at her reaction.

~~~~

The fairgrounds shimmered with lights, creating a magical ambiance as the clock struck 11:59 pm. Prisha stood in the soft glow, her heart beating in rhythm with the anticipation of what awaited her.

"Pata hein aapko ? Hum aapse kitna pyar karte hein?" Said Abhiman looking at her eyes deeply.

Prisha's eyes searched his, a mixture of curiosity and affection dancing in their depths.

"You know i wanted to give you exactly 20 gifts today....

As the clock ticks toward midnight,he continued, "there's one gift left-one that words alone cannot convey."

A minute to midnight, and Abhiman gently cupped prisha's face, his eyes locking onto hers. The world around them seemed to pause, and in that suspended moment, he leaned in. Their lips met in a tender kiss, a culmination of a day filled with love, surprises, and shared moments.

As the clock struck midnight, fireworks painted the sky, illuminating the night in a breathtaking display. Prisha and Abhiman stood, wrapped in each other's arms, amidst the dazzling lights.

"I gave you the gifts that i thought would be best for you. But do you want something else?" He asked.

"Can I really?" She asked, hesitant to voice out her thoughts.

"Hukum karaiye" he said, wanting her to say what she wanted
~~~~

"Do not investigate my past. That monster got what he deserved. Promise me that you won't hurt anybody because of me not even that monster?" She asked

"He didn't get the punishment he deserved. The only punishment he deserved was death, And I will make sure to let him taste the bitter meal named death" he said looking dead serious in her eyes.

"Maan please? For me?" She pleaded.

He sighed

"Why do you want me to stop? Don't you want him to get the punishment he deserves?" I asked her gently.

"I do but...we should just leave this onto kanha ji i trust him enough to let him handle all this" she said looking at Abhiman.

"If that's what you want, but the day I lay my eyes on that fucker, you will find him 10 feets deep inside the ground." He said with seriousness dripping down his tongue.

"You can do anything you want but not until you lay your eyes on him. Ok?" Said prisha.

"Ohk" he said stroking her hair.

"We should get back home right? It's quite late." Prisha stated looking up to the sky. Prisha looked ethereal in the glowing light of the moon.

"If you say so" Abhiman said in agreement.

They reached home and got into their night wears and slept with Abhiman holding prisha in his arms securely.

~~~~~~~~~~~This is it for today guys.
~~~~~~~~~~~

Let me know how this chapter was~

There won't be an update on Saturday as i already posted today.

I love you all □

Byeee~

(NOT AN UPDATE)

Hieeeeeeeeeeeeeee myyyyyyyyyyyyyy goofballssssssssss!!!□□□

Happy new year to all of you □

Hope this new year brings you happiness along with a fictional man for you

I just wanted to inform you all that I will be keeping this story on hold until 20 January because I am on bed rest, your author is really very clumsy, i have a partial tear in my legament. And as i already told you all, I have my exams coming up. To be honest my preparation isn't that good. Hope you understand my perspective. I know some of you might feel that I lack sincerity towards my work, but goofballs i cannot get enough time. I promise to update regularly after 20 January.

Hope you understand my situation and my perspective. That would mean alot to me. □

I love you all soooooooooooo much □ happy new year once again □

~your author

Chapter 25: love?

Thank you all for 80+k reads and 4k+ votes over this book. I never expected that this book would be able to make a place in all your hearts. I just really want to thank you all. Love you all~_________________[Mein parinda besabar Tha uda jo dar-badar Koi mujhko yun mila hai Jese banjare ko ghar....] -banjara_________________PRISHA'S POV

A week has passed for my birthday.......and everything in my life is currently peaceful. I have joined my college again. And he has been going to his company. Nothing has changed between me and Maan......it's as usual. The only thing that has changed is that I have grown even more comfortable around him. I have started opening up to him. I have noticed how happy I get just by exchanging a few words with him. Before I used to shy around him even for uttering a few words. I remember how, initially I couldn't complete any of my sentences without shuttering, and now I wait, wait to have a long conversation with him. He has made his own impact in my life. A positive one. I like these lil changes in my life.

For the past 3 days Maan has been busy with his official works. But he never forgets to take out his time for me. Even if it's little, it's enough for me. But

I am worried for him. He comes a lil later than usual from his work and also seems stressed because of his work. It can also affect his health.

Just see what time it is right now! It's 11pm already!!!!!!!!!!! Huffff-ff!!!!!!!!!!!!!!!

I groaned frustratedly

I have been waiting for him in the hall for the past hour.

"'what should I do? I feel so bored right now!" I mumbled to myself.

"'Oh wait- I can watch something"' I said as I bent a little forward to get a hold on the remote. Debating on what I should watch and what not to, I started watching some random cartoons, while laying on the sofa. As time passed by, my eyes started getting heavy as a result of me falling asleep on the sofa itself.

ABHIMAAN'S POV

I looked over the clock, finding it's already 11:30pm, I let out a deep and exhausted sigh. It's been days that I have been busy like this. And ages since I have had a heartfelt, long convo with prisha. I can hardly make out any time for her...but she never ever complained about anything, let alone complaining she never even asked me about why I am busy, it was me, that I told her myself, that I have been busy with official work at the office. I have noticed these little changes in her, as of how she waits till I get home, waits so that we can eat together, even after I have told her to have her meals on time in case I'm late, but that girl never seems to listen to me. She has started opening up to me, and I am so happy and proud of myself for making her feel comfortable around me. I love the way she tells me about her day. Her voice is the only music I would love to hear without any break or pause. I love the way she tries cooking my fav food for me.

Thinking about this a soft smile played on my lips, unknown to me. That's what the power she holds on me, the Abhimaan singh rajwansh who used to be conscious even during the most unconscious moments, now seems lost even in the right and sane senses.

I chuckled over this thought of mine.

I quickly wrapped up my work and drove my way back home, while humming onto a low melody.

INSIDE THE PALACE~

I walked inside the palace and the guards bowed at me with respect, I just nodded my head at them. Walking inside of the palace, my sight revealed the most adorable sight ever seen by humanity.......... There she is, sleeping adorablely on the sofa, curled up in a ball. While the tv was on. I shook my head at how someone can look so effortlessly adorable and innocent, while doing absolutely nothing?

I walked over the sofa, and knelt down on her level, silently admiring her. Her eyes opened ever so slowly, she blinked them cutely. Aur................ hum pighal gaye humari mohtarma ki is ada par. I looked at her in awe. Her eyes slightly went wide for a sec, before getting back to their normal size. Her hairs!!!!!! They were a barrier between me and her immensely beautifully sculpted face. With my index finger cearesed her lucious locks away, that were falling over her face.

"'Aap abhi tak soyi nahi?" I asked still cearesing her hair gently, though they were not falling over her face anymore.

"'Aap hi ka intezar kar rahe the hun bus'" she lowered her gaze.........maybe due to shyness? She lowered her head looking down on the floor again, causing her hair strands to fall over her face yet again. Here you go again! The fucking hairs. They are annoying me now! Huffffffffff! I yet again removed the hair strands dangling over her face. Looks like I have to deal with this new enemy of mine! That is her hair! How can they get to feel her soft skin? Huffffff! I am jealous now..

"'Isha? Don't get me wrong but can you tie your hair up in a bun or something ?" I asked taking her hands into mine.She lifted her gaze looking at me, she spoke. '"Aapko humare baal acche nahi lage?'"

"'oh my love, it isn't like that it's just'"......... for the first time I felt embarrassed. All because of these hairs of her's. oh how I never felt jealous of anything, but these non-existing things. First that floor that she seems to find the most interesting thing in the world when I am around her. And now her hair.

"'It's just that- that I feel jealous of them." I said looking into her eyes, an amusing made its way to her lips.

"'jealous? Ummm can I ask ,of what?" she asked as the smile was still dancing over her lips. I

"'it's always your long lucious hairs that gets to touch you, they are the ones that I have to fight in order to see your cute yet the 'die for face'. They are the ones I have to fight in the morning to see that beautifully sculpted face of yours, because I want to start and end my day by looking at you. And this stupid hairs always has to hide your face from me.'" I said making her widen her eyes before she bursts into the bubble of laughter. I scrunched my nose cutely looking at her laughing.

"'isha, I am serious here and you are laughing at me'" I faked my anger, folding my hands above my chest.

She stopped laughing after a min or so. She leaned in and cupped my cheeks causing my heartbeat to rise high, maybe up to the sky.

She continued cupping my cheeks and said in a cute tone. 'hume pata nahi tha aap itne cute hein' she Said as she giggled, making an instant smile make its way to my face.

"khana khaya aapne?" I asked, knowing the answer very well.

"'h-hum-bas khane hi wale the'" she said, I knew how fluent of a lie it was. I sighed.

"kitni baar kaha hein hymne aapko, ki khana kha liya kare samye par? Koi sunta kha hein humari?" I said fake glaring at her..

" 'Sorry' she said cutely making an innocent face, making me scrunch my face at her cuteness, ab batao banda gussa bhi nahi ho sakta mohtarma pe, shakal jo itni masoom banati hai humari jaan.

'Aapne khana kaya?" she asked looking at me with a questioning gaze.

'how can i?' I knew it, that you don't eat your meals without me by your side.' I said ceareasing her cheeks.

'rukiye hum khana lagate hein aapke liye' she said as she was about to get up but I pulled her back.

"hum nahi, aap rukiye, hum khana lagayenge aaj' I said getting up from the kneeling position. She held my hand stopping me. I raised my eyebrows looking at her holding my hands, despite the butterflies erupting in my stomach, just by her mere touch.

'par-' I cut her off with a fake glare knowing very well what she was going to say next. Obviously she was going to stop me, my glare, though a fake one made her stop her rant and caused her to pout. Making me chuckle without her noticing.

Leaving her on the sofa I made my way towards the kitchen, heating up our dinner.

PRISHA'S POV

My heart thudded loudly. He cares for me. This thought made thousands of butterflies to enter my stomach. And I don't know why I felt heat hovering over my face. What is happening to me? These symptoms are similar to what Abhishek told me, he said he feels all these when he sees sonam bajawa. And he said it's because he loves her. Oh. That's why. WAIT- WHAT? Do-do-i-I love Maan?

As I was still lost in my thoughts that has been successful in capturing all my attention I didn't notice when Maan was sitting next to me. He snapped his fingers in front of my face. Making me snap out of my thoughts.

"isha? You ok?" he asked looking at me with concerning gaze.

"huh? Oh, yes I am fine.' I replied, though he still wasn't satisfied with my answer but decided to let it slide.

After this we decided to go to the dining room and eat our meal. During the whole time none of us exchanged any words, though he glanced at me quite often. It was all making me feel so shy and timid, and my thoughts from earlier were running inside my mind as a flood. It was disturbing me, my sane side of my mind could make out what I was really feeling Am I really in love with him?

Thinking about all this I dined in silence.

AFTER THE DINNER~

We were now in our room laying beside each other. I was still lost in my thoughts when a voice pulled out of my trance.

"is everything ok meri jaan?' he asked pulling me towards him by my waist.

'jii' I managed to let out a mere mumble.

"'Agar sab sahi mein sahi hai, toh mera radio aaj itna shant kyun hai?" he said referring to the term 'radio' to me, making my eyes go wide, slightly.

"'hawww!! Aap hume radio bol rahe hein?" I said pouting.

'"Nahi to, hum aapko 'humara radio' bol rahe hein."' and that was enough to make me get covered with hues of red. As I was already close to him, my head was almost on his chest, while my legs were Tangled with his. Finding no source to hide my face I decided to hide my face in his chest. Making him chuckle. I felt him snuggling up into the Crook of my neck. He inhaled in my scent.

"I love how you smell, how our heartbeats are Tangled up. I love how your neck is smelling quite like me because of how close we are right now, right behind your neckline and exactly below your hairline. I could breathe you in, until the very last beat of my heart." He said, making my face all red, but he couldn't see it as I was still hiding my face in his chest.

He started cearsing my head, and hummed a slow melody making me feel at peace. My thoughts from earlier faded from my mind. After some mins I was already on the verge of falling asleep. And in no time I fell asleep with me engulfed in his arms.______________________________This is it guysI am not sure about the next update but i am sure it would be after 20 Jan. Vote target 200Until then take care of yourself goofballs □Your author loves you'all □Byee-uu ~~~~~~~~~~~~~~~~~~~~~~

Chapter 26 : Planning

Thank youuuuuu all for 100+k reads.Happy reading ;)~~~~~~~~~~~~~~~~~~~~~~~~~~~~~~~{"Thodi Jagah Dede Mujhe, Tere Paas Kahin Reh Jaaun Main" – Thodi Jagah (Marjaavaan)}~~~~~~~~~~~~~~~~~~~~~~~~~~~~~~~~PRISHA'S POVA peaceful Sunday it is, with my unpleasant thoughts roaming across my mind. I can't understand what I feel for Maan, i really can't.

I was in the kitchen preparing tea for everyone. Being done with it, i asked one of the house helpers to bring the tea outside the lawn. There's Everyone settled outside the house, in the lawn. I too walked towards the lawn.

I settled on the chair beside Maan, yes, he was home today. I forced him to stay at home today. He has been busy for the past few days and i wanted him to relax. So here he is. At home.

Everyone was discussing over some random topics. While i could feel Maan's gaze over me. I bit my inner cheeks to control myself from blushing.

"Bhai-sa it's been ages since we went on a picnic" said Kiara looking at Maan, making him lift his eyes off me.

"Baat to sahi hai" said Yash agreeing with Kiara, they both had a mischievous smile glistening over their faces.

"And?" Maan asked them raising his brow.

"How about we go on a trip ? What say bhabi-sa?" Said Dharya, dragging me in the conversation too, I widened my eyes, they pleaded me to agree through their eyes.

"Umm, it's a nice Idea I guess" I said joining them, the three smiled widely before nodding their heads on my remark.

"Sahi hi keh rahe hein bache, bohot din hue kahi gaye nahi hum sab" said chachi joining our team, we looked over maa and gestured her to join in.

"haan beta, sahi baat hein" said maa giving in, we smiled at her.

Maan sighed, before nodding his head. The three jumped on their places in happiness.

"Ye toh soch lo jana kaha hein?" said papa ji, we all looked over Maan.

"Aap sab mujhe kyun dekh rahen hein? Plan aap sab ka hai decide bhi aap hi sab karen" he said. We all sighed and shook our heads.

"Everyone, what do you all think about Kerala?" said Kiara looking at us for approval, to which Yash immediately shook his head.

"bilkul bhi nahi, yaad nahi tujhe udhaar vo chudail bua rehti hein, jisko humari life mein hunse zayda interest hai. Cancel. Cancel." yash said to which mumma glared at him and we all giggled.

Everybody started discussing where we should go for the picnic.

"bhabi-sa aap hi bata dijiye, humse nahi hora ab decide" said dharya making my eyes go wide.

"hum? Hum kya hi bole ab" I said shrugging off my shoulders. I never was used to getting asked about my thoughts and opinions, it seems new. I always did what I was asked to. As if reading my thoughts, Maan shook his head before saying..

"Ab hum sab vahi jayenge jaha prisha bolengi" he said smirking. I turned to look at him in disbelief and he just shrugged his shoulders.

After a collective pause.......

"ummm how about Shimla?" I hesitated-ly spoke.

"Shimla it is then" he said making the three squeal in happiness, jumping over their place. Everyone was happy and so was I.

"If it's finally I'll go ahead and book the flight tickets" Maan said looking over at me.

"Flight? Hum vaha train se nahi ja sakte? I always Had a wish to travel by train, baba never allowed me." I said softly.

"As you wish Rani saheba, aapka hukum sar aankhon pe" he said chuckling, making an instant smile flash over my face.

~~~~~~~~~~~~~~~~~~~(Later that night~)ABHIMAN'S POV

I was working on my laptop, and Prisha has gone to take a shower. I Heard the water flowing from the shower stop, indicating she is done. And later after a few mins, i sensed foot-steps making me look up at her, oh FUCK. She looks so fuckable in that shirt of mine. Get a grip Abhiman. Control. I inhaled a Deep breath in and let it out. I thought not to look at her because if I did i would end up doing something i would regret later. From the corner of my eyes i could see her combing her hair, reapplying her vermilion. My eyes betrayed me as i found myself stealing glances of her.
~~~~~~~~~~~~~~~~~~~

Somehow getting a grip on myself i started working on the laptop again, but who was i even kidding? I have fucking lost all my concentration. The urge of kissing the life out of her was something that is getting irresistible for me. How can she look so innocent yet activate the dirtiest thoughts in my brain. I think I will have to take a cold shower today.

"Suniyeee?" My chain of thoughts were broken by her voice, my soul is frozen. HOW? How come she has me wrapped up around those tiny fingers of hers, i am so done with my own self now. I am a love sick puppy. But if it's for her do I mind that? Absolutely not.

I cleared my throat before saying "Jii kahiye?".

"Aapka kam hogaya?" She asked.

"Haan, bas lagbhag ho hi Gaya hai." I replied with a soft tone.

"Aap aajkal bohot busy rehte hein, Kam apni jagah hota hai or apni sehat apni jagah.....aur....

"Aur?" I raised my eyebrows wanting to know what she wanted to tell me.

"Agar aap humare sath time nahi spend karenge toh shayad hum aapko bhul bhi sakte hein, humari yaadash bohot kamzor hei."

I chuckled softly at her innocence before saying "Koi nahi, humari yaadash tej hein Hum aapko yaad rakh lenge"

"Umar ho rahi hei aapki, aapki yadash humse bhi kamzor hoti ja rahi hei, time se Ghar aana toh yaad nahi rehta aapko, aye bade hume yaad rakhne wale" she replied sarcastically making my jaw drop on the floor, she's indirectly calling me an old man. Oh, how much I wanted to show her the strength of this old man.

"Aap hume indirectly Budha bol rahi hein?" I asked raising my eyebrows.

"Aap tees ke hone wale hein, that ultimately makes you an oldie right?" She said giggling. Oh fuck i really do have to take a cold shower. I got up from my place taking slow and steady steps towards her, she was still giggling but looking at me coming towards her, her laughter died down her throat. She started taking steps back, her back came in contact with the cold wall, making her halt. I pulled her closer by one hand of mine while the other reached to tuck the hair strand behind her ears, while doing so i leaned in and brought my face closer to her face, leaving barely an inch of a distance.

"Chahe tees ka ho jau ya pachas ka, rahunga toh aapka hi" i said making her lower her gaze, i lifted her chin up by my index finger. She looked into my eyes.

"Thak te nahi aap ye Bollywoody-cheesy lines bolte bolte?" She said with a tint of redness glowing on her cheeks.

"Cheesy lines nahi, pyar hai ye humara, exclusively aapke liye" i said cupping her cheeks gently.

She blushed and hid her face in my chest. I chuckled.

We heard a clearing of throat, the door was shut but wasn't locked, Yash entered the room, making prisha and me straighten up.

"Bhai-sa darwaza mein na lock, room ko lock karne ke liye hota hai" said Yash with a teasing smile.

"Or dimag use karne ke liye hota hai, knock karna ka sense nahi hei?" I replied back with sarcasm dripping down my tongue.

"Inko choro, bhabhi-sa aapko maa ne bolne ke liye kaha he ki kaal aarti ke liye 5 baje uth janeko, kal hum sab mandir jayenge" Yash informed us.

"Vaise you guys can continue, but make sure to lock the door" he said running out of the room.

This brat, I will deal with him tomorrow.I looked beside me only to find my cute biwi burning up in the color of red. I decided to tease her a little.

"So......" I stretched the "so" making her look up at me.

"So?" She asked back confusedly.

"Let us continue what we left?" I said making her eyes go wide. I was an inch away from bursting into a pit of laughing, looking at her reaction.

She fake yawned before saying "bohot raat hogayi hai, nai? She said walking towards the bed. "So Jana chahiye Hume ab, subah uthna bhi toh hai" Saying this she layed down on the bed, pulling the comforter over her, covering her entire self. I chuckled. I walked over the bed i layed down on the other side of the bed.

I pulled her closer to me, making a audible gasp leave her mouth. I slid my hands under the comforter lightly gripping on her waist, i started drawing invisible circles on her waist by my fingers, and before us knowing we both slipped off in the Dreamland.____

__________Next update on Monday Until then take care of yourself Hope you liked the update :)Don't forget to vote and comment. Vote target: 300

Chapter 27: Traveling

READ THIS BEFORE CONTINUING THE CHAPTER---

Hello my lovely goofballs, there's this hate comment i encountered

(""I just don't know why your book is so hyped up and all, I don't feel like you deserve any of it, i have read your story but it was not something new just as any other story, i feel like your story is undeserving. Tbh this story is so boring and stupid, you did not even pair prisha with rudra and paired her up with Abhiman. I hate you for doing this!!!")

{This was the hate comment}

I received this hate comment today! Bhai ek baat suno, if you find my book undeserving then don't read it. It's simple, mein tumhe personally aake nahi bol ri ki meri book padho. I have received 5 such comments earlier too. I choose to ignore it, but Bhai ab bohot hora hai, aur meine clearly mention Kiya hai ki ye ek "love triangle" wala trope hai, usme ab meri thodi galti hai ki tum andho jese use ignore kar rahe ho. Whoever it was i have respectively blocked him/her.

If that person could have asked me normally i would have made a book on rudra's perspective too. But agar tum log yahi karte rahe toh I don't think mein ye story continue karungi. Because it takes EFFORTS to pen down those chapters. If you find this story as any other one, toh phir jao vo book hi padho, meri kyun padh rahe ho? Tumne khud willingly meri book padhi, i did not force you. I swear if i find any other hate comments I'll take down the whole damm book.

Jo log mujhe insta pe follow kartey hai, they know about the whole thing.

And now coming onto my real supporters whom I belovedly call "goofballs" thank you so much for supporting me throughout this journey and always understanding me.

~aapki author~~~~~~~~~~~~~~~~~Happy reading!~~~~~~~~~~~~~~~~~{"Iss chahat mein marr jaaunga, Main phir bhi tumko chahunga"} – Phir Bhi Tumko Chahunga (Half Girlfriend)~~~~~~~~~~~~~~~~~~

ABHIMAN'S POV

(After one week)

We were all done, we all were just going to leave for the station. I looked over at prisha, she was combining her hair pretty aggressively. Aish, at this point she'll just rip off all her hair it seems. I walked over towards her. I tapped on her shoulders, she turned around to look at me. I gestured to her to give the comb to me and she did. Taking the comb in my hands i started combining her hairs. Slowly yet carefully i untangled her hair. Being done with it i started braiding her hair in a French braid.

After 10 mins I was done with it, i kept the comb on the dressing table, she turned around and looked pretty shocked,

"Where did you learn to braid hair?" She asked looking at me with a shocked expression.

"You are forgetting, i have a sister myself, i used to braid her hairs for her" i answered making her nod cutely.

"Let's go now everybody must be waiting" she said making me agree with her statement.

DOWNSTAIRS~

(Author's POV)

As they stepped down they saw all of the other family members were already ready, after keeping the luggage in the back of the car they moved towards the station.

As they reached the station, there was buzzing with the usual hustle and bustle, Abhiman took the family to a platform where literally no one was seen around, Prisha's eyes met his , expressing a mix of gratitude and surprise.

"Bhai-sa idhar toh koi bhi nahi hai lagta hai sab late hogaye Aaj" said Dharya.

"Haina ? Lagta hai sab so rahe hein" said Chachi

"Aisa kuch nahi hai Chachi-sa" Abhiman replied to his Chachi.

"Phir kaisa hai?" Asked papa (Abhiman's dad).

"Humne Puri train book ki hai" Abhiman said shocking everyone as if it wasn't a big deal.

"KYA?" Prisha asked being taken aback.

"Jii, aapne pehli baar humse kuch manga tha, aap chahti thi na ki hum by train travel kare toh i decided to book the entire train for you" he replied

"Oh-hoooooooooooooooooooooooooo" dharya, Kiara and Yash hooted.

"Aap bhi na, itna extraordinary Kam kartey rehtey hai" said prisha palming her forehead and shaking her head a lil.

"Jab humari biwi itni khas hai, toh how do you expect me to do something ordinary?" Abhiman said making dharya Kiara and Yash tease me.

After sometime The train's arrival was announced, and they boarded, finding their fav seats amid the excitement of the journey ahead. Prisha sat beside Abhiman, a subtle smile playing on her lips. The rhythmic sound of the train set a soothing backdrop as we settled in for the ride.

Abhiman, having a flair for grand gestures, had surely surprised Prisha by booking the entire train compartment for our journey.

"Come let me take you somewhere" said Abhiman holding her hand helping her to get up from her seat.

As they stepped into the lavish space, it was adorned with decorations and soft ambient lighting, creating an intimate atmosphere.

Prisha's eyes widened in amazement, "Did you do all of this?"

He grinned, "I thought we could use a more private and special setting for our journey."

The two of them settled into a cozy corner, surrounded by the warmth, there were coming faint noises from the other appartment of the train, probably the trio of Yash Kiara and dharya.

There came a Jerk of the train making prisha stumble on her seat a little, as Abhiman was sitting very closer to her the jerk of the train made her head hit his chest a little, she tried fixing the position, only to find that some of her hair strands were Tangled up with the buttons of his shirt.

Abhiman chuckled as Prisha struggled with her tangled hair. He gently tried to free the strands from the buttons of his shirt, only to get them more Tangled, their eyes meeting in a playful exchange.

"Well, it seems your hair has its own plans for this journey," Abhiman teased prisha .

Prisha blushed, "Looks like it."

After sometime of struggle they were able to free the strands away from the grasp of buttons.

With that prisha mumbled a small yet a low "thank you" and was about to scoot away from him he pulled her closer, he grabbed onto her waist and pulled her on his lap.

"Ye-ye a-ap kya ka-r ra-he hei-n" she said widening her eyes.

"Apni biwi ke sath romance, koi pareshani mohtarma?" With that he crashed his lips onto hers.

After a good minute he parted away, he looked into her eyes before snuggling up in the Crook of her neckline, he inhaled her, making her heart do a backflip. His hold onto her tightened, her heartbeat was racing wildly, a sane part of her was telling her that it was wrong, while the other insane part of her was craving of his touch. She could not bring herself to stop him, neither now or she can in the future,

because.........she is developing feelings for him, unaware of it herself.Wit hout any other thought, Abhiman slightly bit on her neckline. Making a foreign sound escape her lips. He nibbled onto it for a while and parted away from her neck. They both were breathing insanely, she looked down and said more like whispered "Maan not now, we are on a train" she said as she lowered her eyes, she breathed heavily with the burning intensity of his gaze she felt on herself.

"Exactly meri jaan, we are on a train. You better be quiet." He said smirking, making her jaw drop on the floor.

MEANWHILE~

Yash was roaming around, he found lights coming out of a certain compartment, he went in to inform Kiara and dharya about it.

"Sunnnnnnnnnnno, ek compartment mein se lights AA Rahi hein, koi chor toh nahi aagaya?" Yash expressed.

"Abey gadhe, chor kya electrician hai jo lights leke ghumega?" Dharya said sarcastically, Yash gaped at him.

"Tune mujhe ghadha bola?" Yash asked raising his eyebrows at dharya.

"Tu hai, tujhe pata nahi par tu hai" Dharya replied back with the same time of sarcasm.

"Ruk Teri toh mein complain bhabhi-sa se karunga" said Yash keeping both his hands on his waist.

"Ja karle complain, vaise bhi bhabhi-sa mujhse zyada pyaar karti hai, tujhe toh bas bura na lag Jaye is liye thoda bohot baat kar leti hai tujh jaise uncultured bandar se" dharya said, on his remark Yash scoffed.

"Udna band kar bhabhi-sa mujhse zyada pyaar karti hai" Yash said pointing his forefinger at dharya.

"TU-" dharya was cut off in between by Kiara.

"Shut up you both, na bhabi-sa Yash tujh se pyar karti hai na hi dharya tujhese, meri bhabhi-sa sirf aur sirf mere Abhiman bhai-sa se pyar karti hai." Said Kiara in a very calm tone.

"Poin toh hai" said both Yash and dharya while nodding their heads.

"Ab Jake dekhe hei kya us compartment mein?" Asked Kiara to both of them and they agreed walking towards the compartment.

The trio of Yash, Kiara, and Dharya, curious about the commotion, peeked into the decorated compartment. They were shocked to witness the scenario infront them, because Abhiman and prisha was sitting in a very ***ahem ahem*** wala position.

"HAWWWWWWWWWWWWWWWWWW" yelled Kiara sttraling prisha and Abhiman.

"Oh fuck. Tum teeno mujhe kabhi baap Banne ka sukh galti se bhi prapt mat hone dena" he said making prisha as red as a tomato. He continued.

"jabhi bhi kuch karun tum teeno mein se koi ek prakat ho hi jata hai, aur aaj prisha ke kanha ji ki kripa se tum teeno ke teeno sath? Wah wah."

"Shant Bhai shant. Humko laga koi chor hai. Is compartment mein lights thi na isliye" said Yash.

"Arey wah chor electrition kab se ban gaye?" He asked with a sarcastic smile.

"SAME. Meine bhi yahi pucha is gadhe se" said dharya smaking Yash's head.

"Btw ye compartment zyada accha hai, we'll stay here only" said Yash, Abhiman was about to reply but prisha palmed his mouth.

"Han, Han mujhe bhi company mil jayegi, you guys stay here we have no problem" prisha said getting off Abhiman's lap.

"First of all there's no "WE" it's solely your decision to let these three monkeys stay here. And second of all what do you mean by "mujhey bhi company mil jayegi" what am I? Am i invisible or something?" Asked

Abhiman raising his eyebrows at prisha who looked out of words right now.

"Bhai you gotta admit it that you are pretty boring, even bhabhi-sa is bored of you now" Yash said and giggled but it died down his throat when he saw Abhimaan shooting a glare his way.

"Arey mein toh mazak kar raha tha" said Yash scratching his nape.

"Chalo hum sab antakshari khel te hein" prisha said in a attempt to devert their mind.

They all agreed and played a lot of games. The journey unfolded with a blend of shared moments, laughter, and the occasional train sway. Abhiman's grand gesture had set the tone for a memorable journey, and as they traveled and played until late at night, before eventually falling asleep. ~~~~~~~~~~~~~~~~~~~~~That's it for today!

Comment down your thoughts.

And do follow me on Instagram, i post about the updating schedule there, and sometimes I post spoilers too!

Aur, i don't know about when will be the next update because honestly speaking i have lost all my motivation, but when I'll be done writing the new chapter I will post it right away.!

Thank you

Take care of yourself until the next update!

Vote target: 350~~~~~~~~~~~~~~~~~~~~~~~~~~~~~~~~~~~~~~~

Chapter 28: Shimla's charm

Hieeeeeeeeeeeeeeeee my goofballssssssssss □Thank youuuuuu for 150k+ reads! Never have I ever been so grateful!I know I am being so inactive nowadays, but i swear I'll be updating regularly from now on! I will be uploading on every Saturday. ~~~~~~~~~~~~~~~~Is chapter mein mein Inka trip khatam karva dungi, because mere dimag mein kuch aa nahi Raha hai (Author ka dimag Khali hai, kuch nahi bacha ab)

And prisha's POV in this chapter has my heart! Do comment on what you felt about her POV>3________________________{"Hawaa ke jaise chalta hai tu, Main ret jaisi udti hoon, Kaun tujhe yun pyar karega, Jaise main karti hoon" – Kaun Tujhe (MS Dhoni: The Untold Story)}________________________AUTHOR'S POV

The train's rhythmic motion lulled them into a peaceful sleep, the compartment filled with the soft hum of the moving wheels. As they journeyed through the night, the group of Abhiman prisha, and the trio, while the oldies were enjoying themselves in the other compartment and family found comfort in each other's company, creating memories that would last a lifetime.

Being tired of playing continuously the youngsters seemed very tired, Prisha was way too tired to even move a limb, she fell asleep on Abhiman's shoulder itself. Yash Kiara and dharya too got up and left for their own fav compartments. While Abhiman also carried prisha to her compartment. And he himself went for his compartment.

Abhiman, kept going to prisha's compartment to check up on her because obviously he cannot even spend a minute without her let alone being away from her for the whole night.

As the night unfolded, the train carried them through landscapes of dreams, and amidst the gentle sway of the compartments, they embraced the beauty of the unexpected moments that life bestowed upon them.

NEXT MORNING

(Author's POV)

The train gradually slowed down as it approached Shimla, waking up the Abhiman and the from his night's slumber. The first rays of the sun painted the sky in hues of pink and orange, casting a warm glow on the picturesque landscapes outside.

Abhiman stepped into prisha's compartment, walking towards her, as they have reached to their destination. He walked towards her shaking her gently.

"Meri jaan, uth jaiye hum puhonch Gaye hein" he said stroking her hair gently making her open her eyes gently.

"Hum puhonch Gaye?" She asked straightening up and rubbing her eyes cutely.

"Ji mohtarma" he said chuckling at her cute lil movements.

Hearing upon him she held his hand and walked out of her compartment, to where all other members were.

As they stepped off the train onto the Shimla station platform, the crisp mountain air greeted them. The temperature was noticeably cooler than what they had experienced on their journey. Shimla, with its colonial architecture and the scent of pine in the air, welcomed them with open arms.

"Hayeeee kitni pyari hawa chal Rahi hai! Heina bhabhi-sa?" Dharya asked prisha making her nod her head repeatedly with a wide smile over her face.

"Heina? Kina Sona nazara hai" prisha said admiring the view.

"Ji, Behad pyara" Abhiman replied looking at her, he absolutely loved what he was looking at.

"Oho Bhai, kal toh humne disturb kar Diya tha, pakka wala promise, aaj nahi karenge." Yash said giggling with the other two, the three of them had a sinister Smile over their faces.

"Kya disturb hua tha kal?" Abhiman's father asked making a shy smile crept over prisha's face.

"Arey dad voh-" Yash was cut off when Abhiman glared at him, making him gulp hardly.

"Kiara bataegi" Yash said pointing at Kiara making her wide her eyes

"Mein? Mein kya bolu? Dharya batayega!" Kiara said instantly.

"Mein toh soya hua tha mujhe kuch nahi pata, bhabhi-sa aap boliye na" dharya said making everyone's head turn in the detection of prisha.

Prisha widened her eyes and said "hu-m? Voh-actu-ally-

"Beta saaf saaf bolo" Abhiman's Chachi said.

"Voh Maan na mujhe kal dant rahe the toh Yash Kiara aur dharya vaha aagaye, toh voh abhi isliye sorry bol rahe they ki unhone disturb kar diya." Prisha lied and blabbered something to which Abhiman's mother glared at Abhiman and walked towards Abhiman.

Abhiman's mother gestured to Abhiman to lower his head a lil, he obliged. She rotated his ears saying "himmat kaise Hui Teri meri phool si bacchi ko dantne ki? Meri bacchi itni maasoom hai, itni pyari hai, aur tu nalayak use dant Raha hai? Tu ghar chal ek baari mein tujhe bataun ki dant hoti kya hai!" She screamed at him and rotated his ears making him hiss in pain.

"Mumma bas kariye na unhe lag jayegi" prisha said not being able to see him in pain.

"Unhe? Oh-hoooooooooooooooooooooooo" dharya Kiara and Yash hooted.

"Dekh nalayak abhi bhi tujhe bacha Rahi hai meri bacchi, aur tu nalayak use dant Raha tha ghor kalyug, ghor kalyug" Chacchi said hitting him lightly over his arms.

"Arey maa bas bhi kariye ab, lag rahi hai" Abhiman said grumbling in pain, as his mother still hasn't left his ears.

"Lagne ke liye hi kar rahi hai vo" Abhiman's father said with a slay smirk over his face.

"Meri beti ko ab tu dant kar dekh, phir batata hun ek baap apni beti ke liye kya kya kar sakta hai" Abhiman's father said as he rolled his sleeves.

"Mummaaaaa ab toh chor dijeye unhe" prisha pleaded making his mother leave him, while Abhiman fake glared at her, making her hold her ears and mumble an inaudible "sorry".

"Ab mujhe dant kar hogaya ho toh chalen?" Abhiman asked everyone making them nod their heads.

Abhiman led the group towards their accommodation for the stay, a quaint cottage nestled amidst the hills. The panoramic view from the cottage took their breath away, and the tranquility of the surroundings added to the charm of their retreat.

Abhiman and prisha came inside of their cottage, Abhiman closed the door behind and leaned on to the door, folding his arms over his chest.

"Han toh aap kya bol rahin thi bahar mohtarma?" Abhiman asked folding his arms over his chest.

"Kuch bhi toh nahi" Abhiman raised his eyebrows hearing upon this.

"Aaccha ji?" he asked stepping closer to her.

"Ji" prisha said taking steps back.

"Samajhti kya hein aap khudko?" Abhiman asked caging her in between his arms.

"Aapki Dharm patni, Prisha Abhiman Singh Rajwansh" Prisha said while looking into his eyes.

"Aur Mr. Aap khudko kya samajhte hein? Aap hume humesha ese diwar or aapke bich mein sandwich banane mein lag hote hein" Prisha huffed.

"Aapka pujniya pati dev, Abhiman Singh Rajwansh." Abhiman mimicked her tone from earlier.

"Hawww meri billi mujhiko meow?" Prisha said folding her hands over her chest.

"Ji han ye Billota aapka hi hai" Abhiman said smirking making her roll her eyes.

"Aap bhi na pura din flirting kartey rehtey hain" Prisha said making a frustrated face.

"Kya hi Karen ab, aap bhi toh pure din itni khubsurat dikhti hein" Abhiman replied back chuckling at her frustrated face.

"Kitne dheet hote jas rahe hein aap, ese rahenge toh koi bhi pasand nahi karega aapko!" Prisha said.

"Logo ka toh pata nahi, aap bataiye aapko kaisa lagta hun?" Abhiman asked smirking making Prisha even more frustrated

"Aapke pass koi kaam nahi hein?" Prisha exclaimed looking at Abhiman.

"Ab aapse bepanah mohabbat karna aur aapke nakhre uthana hi mera kaam hai, or kuch kaam karvana ho toh bataiye madam?" Abhiman whispered huskily bending down a lil just front of her ears.

"Aap kitne dheet hein!" Prisha said scrunching her nose cutely.

"Aur aap swarg se utri Hui kokil kanthi aapsara hein" Abhiman said chuckling as he was enjoying teasing her.

"AISHHHH, side hatiye aap" Prisha said to which his smirk widened.

"Na hatun toh?" Abhiman asked.

"Mein ro dungi" prisha said frustratedly, one thing about her, she cries When she's happy she cries When she's sad, she cries when she's frustrated, and she she cries over anything.

"Arey Mera baccha, ese na Karo hum hat rahein hein, aap ab thodi der aaram kar lijiye, thak gayi hongi aap" Abhiman immediately said stepping aside, scared she might actually start crying.

"Hum shower leke aayenge uske baad soyenge" she said as she started walking towards the bathroom.

"Aap aaram kar lijiye tab tak" prisha said walking inside the bathroom closing the door behind.

"Mohtarma humari Jaan lengi ek din" Abhiman mumbled keeping a hand over his chest.

Abhiman layed down on the bed, waiting for Prisha but fell asleep while doing so.

PRISHA'S POV(After 25 mins)I stepped out of the bathroom, while drying my hairs, i looked over the bed, only to find him already asleep. I walked towards the bed. I kept the towel on the table before sitting next to him.

He looked so peaceful while sleeping, he's just so pure and selfless isn't he? He cares for me like the way i care for my loved ones, he loves me like the way fictional men love their female leads and he looks at me like I am some kind of a gem. But in reality he's the real gem, a rare one, the one only I can have.

I gently caressed his cheeks, i bent forward and planted a soft kiss over his forehead.

I know I am losing myself in the pit of his love, but I don't regret it, not a bit. Instead i love how he has turned me into a new different person. A person who belongs to him, and only him.

Thinking about all these i got up and dried down my hairs before laying down on the bed, and falling asleep while snuggling closer to him.

~~~~~~~~~~~~~~~~~~~~~AUTHOR'S POV Throughout their stay, they explored the vibrant markets of Shimla, tasted local delicacies, and indulged in the cultural richness of the region. The journey that had begun with a grand gesture on a train continued to unfold into a tapestry of shared experiences and deepening connections.
~~~~~~~~~~~~~~~~~~~~~

In the evenings, they gathered around a bonfire, sharing stories and laughter against the backdrop of the starlit sky. Prisha found herself drawn to Abhiman's warmth, the bond between them evolving beyond the ordinary.

Shimla's enchanting beauty acted as a catalyst for self discovery and the realization of emotions that had taken root during their journey. Abhiman, with his genuine gestures and Prisha, with her infectious laughter, created a harmonious symphony that echoed in the serene hills of Shimla.

As they bid farewell to Shimla, the memories they forged remained etched in their hearts. The return journey on the train was accompanied by a sense of fulfillment, carrying back a piece of Shimla's charm, a charm that had woven its way into the fabric of their shared experiences.

The train chugged away, carrying them back to their routine lives, but the journey had left an indelible mark, a mark of love, laughter, and the magic that happens when hearts intertwine on a scenic journey through life.____________________________________That's it for today!Hope you liked it□!Love you□!Take care of yourself until the next update.Do vote and comment!Vote target 400 Byeeeyeyeyeyeyeyeyeyeyeyeyeyeyeiiii-iiiiiiiiiiiiiiiiiiiiii ______________________________

Chapter 29: destiny's dirty game

HIEEEEEEEEEEEEEEEE MYYYYYYYYYYYYYY GOOFBALLSSSSSSSSS!!!!!!!!!!!Thank youuuuuu s o o o o o o o o o o o o o o o o o o o o o o o o o o o muchhhhhhhhhhhhhhhhhhhhhhhh for 200k reads and 11k+ votes!!!!~~~~~~~~~~~~~~~~~~~~~~~~Aaj tumhari Author tum sab ko trauma degi! Tissue paper leke betho□(Author khud likhte likhte 2 ghante roi hai)Sorry in advance bohot emotional update hai ye!~~~~~~~~~~~~~~~~~~~~~~~~{"Iss chahat mein marr jaaunga, Main phir bhi tumko chahunga" – Phir Bhi Tumko Chahunga (Half Girlfriend)}~~~~~~~~~~~~~~~~~~~~~~~~(Sensitive people can skip this chapter)

PRISHA'S POV

Hufffff what a hectic day it was! College really does tire me! I took a deep breath and gulped down a glass of water, i sat down over the bed.

Today i feel content enough to know that Maan is the person i would be grateful to spend my life with. I am not confused over my feelings, nor do i doubt if I love him or not. I know THAT I LOVE HIM. I am not hopelessly in love with him, i am hopefully in love with him.

Today's the day I'll be confessing my love for him. He has the right to know how madly deeply and senselessly i am in love with him. I love him. I love him. I love him. And I'll never be tired of saying this.

I got up from the bed and walked over the wardrobe, taking out a red coloured saree, after doing so i walked inside of the bathroom and took a long shower.

Coming out of the shower I wore the saree, wore my favourite jhumka and matching glass bangles. Being done with it, i sat in front of the mirror and took a hold of my makeup supplies. I, for the first time wore a very bright red lipstick.

I was done doing my makeup. I wore my mangalsutra and took the sindur daan in my hands, (bottle of vermillion), i was about to apply it but unfortunately it slipped off my palms, making it scatter all over the floor.

I widened my eyes looking at the floor, i bent over and started collecting the scattered vermilion, once Sneha di told me that it's a sign of a bad omen, i kept a palm over my heart and silently prayed to God for everyone's safety. To calm my racing thoughts i started thinking about something else.

Well it's been 3 months since we visited Shimla, hayeeee kitna pyara tha udhar sab, thinking about this I took a hold over my phone.

I opened my phone, and took a look at the notifications, I saw about 4-5 notifications and none of it was from Maan. I was about to text Maan before i could, my phone rang, displaying "Bhai " over the screen.

I smiled and answered it, it's been almost a week , since i last had a conversation with Bhai.

"Hello?" I said as soon as i answered the call.

"Hii mera baccha! Kaisi hai?" Bhai asked in his usual calm tone.

"Jii Bhai hum toh bohot acche hein, aap sunaiye ? Aap kaise hein? Maa aur baba kaise hein?" I bombarded him with tons of questions.

"Shant meri rail gaadi, shant. Hum sab bohot acche hein, par...." Bhai took a pause while I waited for him to complete his sentence, but on the other side I got nothing but silence.

"Boliye na bhai? Hume chinta ho Rahi hai" I exclaimed as i felt my heart-beat race faster.

"Voh-" he took a collective pause while here I felt my heart coming out of its ribcage.

"Bolen na bhai!!" I pleaded helplessly.

"Sneha vapas aa gayi" Bhai enclosed the factor making me somewhat anxious.

"Aur?" I asked lowly, merely a meek whisper.

"Voh- Ba-ba" i felt bhai's voice break up a little making me even more anxious than I was before.

"Baba? Baba ko kya hua? Bhai mujhe dar lag raha hai bolen na? Please?" I pleaded as i felt my cheeks wet, as of how my tears were flowing.

"Sne-ha ne sha-di kar li! Ba-ba y-e de-kh n-ahi pa-ye Bab-a ko he-art att-ack Aya hai" he finally told me breaking down, making my heart sink into my stomach, i stumbled and took the support of nearby wall in order to keep myself standing, failing to do so i dropped down my knees.

"B-hai n-a ka-ren es-a maz-ak, na kar-en B-hai" A sob escaped my lips, i broke down completely.

"Pri mera baccha meri baat sun, tu toot jayegi toh baba ko kon sambhalega ? Pata hai na tujhe vo tere alawa kisi ki nahi sunte? Abhishek bas udhar pohonchta hi hoga, vo tujhe Airport pe milega, tu udhar pohounch ja, baba tujhe dekhna chahta hein" Bhai told me and i nodded my head agressively and wiped away my tears harshly. (Ps: Abhishek 2 ghante pehle flight mein betha tha, i don't know ki proper kitne ghante lagte hein Rajasthan Jane ke liye, just a random guess)

"Ji-i Bh-ai" i shuttered as i said those words.

"Dhayn rakh" saying this he hung up the call making me blankly state at the screen, tears shamelessly flowing out of my eyes, lipstick smeared over my face, sweat beads covering my forehead.

I broke down once again in the bubble of tears, "I can't lose my baba, he's my hope, my father, my protector, my ray of hope, my strength, my weakness in short my everything. I can't lose him. He was always there for me, i can't lose my baba, i can't lose him at any cost" i screamed as I racked my fingers through my hairs, making them match my appearance, All Messy.

After mins of sobbing i tried to get up, fortunately succeeded in doing so, not caring about my appearance i stepped out of my room, walking straight to the dining hall, as everyone would be there to have their dinner.

"Meri bacchi kya hua? ye kya haal bana liya hai tune?" Chacchi said as soon as she noticed me.

"Laddoo kya hua? Bol beta?" Mumma said coming towards me running as she heard chacchi say.

"Mu-m-ma" my lips wobbled and tears made their way out of my eyes once again, looking at me shuttering mumma embraced me in her arms, making a painful sob escape my lips.

"Shhhh shant, mein hun na?-" mumma was cut off when papa said "sirf Teri mumma nahi, hum sab tere sath hei gudiya, tu bol toh sahi hua kya?"

"Han beta bol toh? Hua kya meri rajkumari?" Chaccha ji asked me while Yash Kiara and dharya came towards me with hurried steps.

"Voh-Ba-ba k-o he-art att-ack a-aya h-ai" i exclaimed earning gasps in return, mumma started patting my back providing me some strength.

"Mujh-e airp-ort le chale-in pleas-e? Abhis-hek Mer-a ud-har wa-it kar Ra-ha hai" i pleaded choking onto my own tears, making everyone's eyes wet.

"Han bhabhi-sa, aap hukum kariye. Aap humari bhabhi-sa hein, aur hum sab ki rani-sa, aap ese himmat nahi haar sakti" dharya said while the other two nodded.

"Mein bhabhi-sa ko airport chor ke aata hun" Yash said wiping his own tears.

"Tu fikar mat kar meri Ladoo, sab theek ho jayega" mumma said wiping my tears, i straightened myself.

"Aur apne luggage ki tension mat le, mein pack karva ke bhijwa dungi" Chacchi said as she hugged me once before parting away.

"Chal ab, meri sherni hai na tu? Ro mat gudiya" papa said and hugged me making me feel exactly the same as of how I felt whenever i hugged my baba.

"I know you got this bhabhi-sa!" Kiara said while i nodded, because I was not in the state to even mumble anything.

Taking everyone's blessings and bidding goodbyes, i left for the airport with Yash.~~~~~~~~~~~~~~~~~~~~~~~~~~~~~AT THE AIRPORT~As soon as i reached there, Yash opened the car's door for me. I came out of it.

"Bhabi-sa be strong! Apna khayal rakhna, sab theek ho jayega" Yash said engulfing me in a hug.While i meekly nodded.

"Suno? Maan ko kuch mat batana abhi, jab ghar aajaye vo tab aaram se batana, Aaj unki important deal hai, mujhe pata hai ki agar tum unhe, abhi bataoge toh voh meeting chor ke aa jayenge" i said lowly, not having enough energy.

"Bhabi-sa mein aapko promise toh nahi kar sakta, kyunki ye baat sabko pata hai ki vo aapse kitna pyar kartey hein, agar humne ye baat chupai toh unka gussa aap bhi nahi sambhal payengi" Yash said helplessly.

"Theek hai, tum aapna aur baki sabka dhyan rakhna" i said patting his cheeks.

"Aap bhi" Yash said as i turned around getting inside of the airport, i aimlessly started walking.

"PRI" i heard someone yell out my name, i lifted my blood shot eyes to find Abhishek standing there, i ran as fast as i could. I landed in his arms. My tears again started flowing like water flows from the river.

He took me into his arms and started patting my back in order to comfort me.

"Y-e sa-b kyu-n hu-a, Abhi?" I asked hiccuping and lightly hitting his chest, sobbing inconsolable.

"Shant hoja pri, uncle ko kuch nahi hoga, tu bharosa rakh" he said as hi parted away and we left for our flight.~~~~~~~~~~~~~~~~~~~~~~~AB HIMAN'S POVI was in between the meeting but all my thoughts were engaged in her thoughts. Sighing i opened up my phone and texted her.

Minutes passed but i got no reply, i frowned, because she replies to each and every one of my texts within 5 mins.

I felt a bit uneasy at this thought of mine, i instantly dialled her number, with each passing ring I felt my heartbeat race faster. After 4 rings of it, Someone picked up the call.

"Hello" i heard Yash say on the other side of the phone. My frown deepens.

"Prisha ka phone tere pass kaise aaya?" I asked ignoring his "hello".

"B-bhai-sa voh-voh-na-actu-ally" he fumbled onto his words, making it clear that Something was off.

"Yash i asked you a simple daam question. What is prisha's mobile phone doing with you?" I asked , darkening my eyes.

"Voh bhai-sa-" i cut him off in between. "And dare you to lie" i threatened him.

"Bhabi-sa" he paused in between his sentence.

"PRISHA KO KYA HUA HAI?" I yelled I screamed over the phone as i lost every ounce of patience i was holding onto. My scream strategized everyone present in the meeting room.

Yash being a scaredy cat, narrated the entire daam thing. Making my eyes turn blood red, as i imagined isha's stricken face.

"Aur bhabhi sa jate jate aapna phone bhul gayi car mein" he finished off.

"ITNA SAB HOGAYA AUR KISINE MUJHE KUCH KYUN NAHI BATAYA? HUH?" I roared in pure rage.

"Bhai-sa hu-me bha-bhi-sa ne m-ana Kiy-a th-a" Yash shuttered clearly scared of my anger.

"TUM SAB KO MEIN UDHAR AAKAR BATATA HUN" i yelled I felt the veins of my forehead popping out, because of the intensity of my anger.

Getting up, i started walking away from the meeting hall, that's when I heard my assistant say "Sir what about this meeting?" He asked making me turn around i looked at him with all my fury, i replied "Fvk that meeting off, for all i care" saying this I walked out.

Getting inside of my car, i started driving recklessly, i know how sensitive she is, I don't know how would she have handled this news. And the damn fact that none of them cared to tell me anything.

i started racing the car faster, not caring about the speed limit anymore, the only thing I care about is my love, Something that I hate about her , is her tears, that is the sole thing that I hate about her and will continue to do so until my last breath. I felt my own eyes watering imagining her wailing like a child, she turns into a complete baby while crying. Meri jaan i am sorry, I was not there for you when you needed me the most.

Out of nowhere, a truck came in my sight, i widened my eyes, looking at it coming in my direction.

And.......

The truck collided with my car, making my car flip over, the glasses of my car scattered into pieces, and they pierced deep inside my skin.The wreckage left me trapped between shattered glass and twisted metal, my body aching from the impact. As the blaring sirens approached, my thoughts oscillated between the immediate pain and the haunting worry for Isha. Before losing my consciousness I felt people taking me out of the car, and taking me to the hospital.

MEANWHILE~(AUTHOR'S POV)All the family members (Abhiman's family) were sitting gloomy-ly as they have witnessed such a painful state of Prisha. All the family members were veryyyyyyy very close to her, it's like she has become a peice of their heart.

Dharya's phone rang diverting all there attention to his phone. Dharya looked at the phone screen, it was from a unknown number, nevertheless he picked it up.

Not until hearing the news the other person enclosed over the phone's other side of it. Dharya's phone dropped.

"Kya hua? Ladoo ka phone tha?" Abhiman's mother asked.

"Maa bhai-sa ka accident ho gaya hai" dharya said shocking everyone to their core.

"KYA?" Abhiman's mother yelled.

"Kaha hei Mera baccha? Mujhe uske pass le chal, Abhiman ke papa le chalen mujhe mere bacche ke pass" Abhiman's mother broke down into tears.

All the family members of Rajwansh family retarted to the given address of the hospital.~~~~~~~~~~~~~~~~~~~~~~~~~~~PRISHA'S POV

We got off the plane, we sat there for a while waiting for Bhai to come pick us up.

I looked around to find my phone, i atleast wanted to text Maan. Not finding the phone i frowned.

Holly heavens i forgot my phone in the car only! How will I text Maan now? Oh i have Abhishek's phone too right? I should at least call him and inform him.

Asking for Abhishek's phone i dialled Maan's number. It said that the phone was switched off.I felt a bit uneasy, and anxiety took over me. I was already very disturbed and now him not picking my phone calls were making me anxious.

Feeling anxious I called Kiara, she picked up the call, i could hear someone crying, this just added fuel to my worries.

"Kiara? Maan Ghar pochene?" I asked hoping she'll answer positively instead I heard a sorrowful sob.

"Bha-bi-sa, Bhai-sa dekhe na uth nahi rahe hein" Kiara said as she hiccuped, i felt something inside my heart crumble.

"Ye kya bol rahi ho Kia? Ese mazak acche nahi hote" i scolded her, wanting her to say it's just a lie.

"Mein sach bol rahi hun bhabi-sa, Bhai-sa ka accident ho gaya" and that was what took me to break down in the pit of tears yet again. Seeing me Abhishek took the phone off of my hands. My hands Shivered.

I wanted her to tell me it was a joke, I wanted her to tell me she was just fooling around with me. Please tell me it's a joke please! I beg you! Please! This can't be happening! This can't be happening, when i thought everything was at it's rightfull place, why did this had to happen! WHY? I love him, i love him, i love him. Mera dam ghut Raha hai, mein nahi reh paungi unke bina, esa lag raha hai jaise koi Mera gala ghot Raha ho. mein mar jaungi.

"Kya hua pri?" Abhishek asked me instead of replying i hugged him, because "I wanted someone to tell me it's all a damm lie. at this point I don't want anything except for my Maan.I sobbed clutching onto his collar. I sobbed as if it's the end of the world. I love him. When I was about to confess why did this have to happen? WHY? Destiny cannot be this cruel. Destiny has snatched away my first love, and now this? NO! I cannot let destiny play that dirty game again." I thought as I cried more and more. I want my Maan.

I am nothing without him. Nothing without his presence. Nothing without his love. My existence roams around HIM.

~~~~~~~~~~~~~~~~~Destiny cannot be this cruel or.......can it be? What will happen to Primaan? Unseen forces had collided in the intersection of their lives, mirroring the chaos that unfolded on the dimly lit road .~~~~~~~~~~~~~~~~~That's it for today!Tum logo ko pehli baar clif hanger pe chor Rahi hun!Meri aankhe dukh Rahi hai rote rote Mein ja rahi hun soneTum sab bhi so jao Vote target 400Aur Han guys mein aaj jaldi update Kiya hai aur ye update bohot bada bhi hai toh i guess ab mein direct Monday update karungi! Love you all ;)Take care until the next update!Stay tuned:)~~~~~~~~~~~~~~~~~~
~~~~~~~~~~~~~~~~~

Chapter 30: Cruel

- -

Hiee my goofballs! How are you'all doing? I hope you guys are doing fine!So the thing is i want to thank each one of you who supported me throughout this journey!Thank you all for choosing this book, never in my wildest thoughts did I think that this book will achieve something but here is this book, that achieved more than what I desired and it happened only because you love and support because you choose this book. I am truly greatful to each one of you.

(Aaj ka update bohot chota hai, but agala update bada hoga, i promise!) ~~~~~~{"Bekhayali Mein Bhi Tera Hi Khayal Aaye, Kyun Bichhadna Hai Zaroori Ye Sawaal Aaye" – Bekhayali (Kabir Singh)}~~~~~~PRISHA'S POV

Kya hua pri?" Abhishek asked me instead of replying i hugged him, because "I wanted someone to tell me it's all a damn lie. at this point I don't want anything except for my Maan.I sobbed clutching onto his collar. I sobbed as if it was the end of the world. I love him. When I was about to confess why did this have to happen? WHY? Destiny cannot be this cruel. Destiny has snatched away my first love, and now this? NO! I cannot let destiny play that dirty game again." I thought as I cried more and more. I want my Maan.

I am nothing without him. Nothing without his presence. Nothing without his love. My existence roams around HIM.

"Bol Naa kya hua, mujhe tension ho Rahi hai!" Abhishek asked me while gently patting my back.

"Maan-ka acc-ident ho-gaya" i cried out my heart.

"KYA?" He screamed, out of shock. Making me sob more.

"Shhh chup hoja, tu aise thodi himmat har sakti hai, Agar Abhiman idhar hora toh tujhe rota dekh ke use accha lagta?" Abhishek asked me trying to console me, but how could you expect me to calm down? My life has turned into a complete and an absolute mess. First Baba and now this.

"Idhar dekh" Abhishek exclaimed holding my shoulders and making me look up to him.

"Bhagwan na kare, but agar Tera accident ho jata, aur Abhiman ese rota toh tujhe accha lagta?" Abhishek asked making my vision blur with tears as i imagined him crying. It broke a part of me to even think about it.

"Bol?" Abhishek shook my shoulders lightly.

"N-ahi, ye soc-h k-ar hi me-ra Dil Tut Ra-ha hai." I replied back to him. He smiled.

"Toh use kaise lagega jab use pata chalega ki tu aise ro rahi hai? Tujhe strong bana hoga pri" he tried making me understand while i nodded my head.

I kept my head on his shoulder feeling exhausted, we started waiting for bhaiya to come and pick us up i kept praying for both baba and Maan. Abhishek was right. I need to be strong.

After a while Bhai came. I got up from my seat as i saw sneha di coming along with Bhai.

Tears of anger collected inside my eyes.

Sneha di stood in front of me, she tried to hug me but i stepped back, not looking into her eyes.

"Pri? Bacche kaise hai tu?" Di asked me trying to cup my cheeks but I pushed her hand away.

"Kyun aaye ho aap ab? Huh? Sab bigad ke rakh diya aapne. Sab." I exclaimed looking at her with anger in my eyes.

"I am sorry bacche i did not have any choice" she said trying to convince me but i was in no state to understand or to listen to her.

"Ek baar mujhe bol dete aap, mein baat karti baba se, vo Man jaate" i said.

"I am sorry pri" she replied.

"Kis baat ke liye sorry bol rahe ho aap? US baat ke liye jab Aap shadi chor ke chale gaye? Us baat ke liye jab baba ko aapke vajah se Maan ke aage mafi mangni padi ? Us baat ke liye ki aapne Hume itne dino se contact nahi kiya? Ya phir us baat ke liye ki aapki vajah se baba is halat mein hein?" I finally lost it. I yelled at her while tears brimmed out my eyes. She had tears collected inside her eyes.

"Maaf nahi karegi aapni bhen ko?" She asked while tears spilled out from both our eyes.

Saying this she hugged me, i did not resist this time. We both cried onto each other's embrace. She's my sister After all one day or another i have to forgive her. I do not hate her or anything. Nor did I mean anything I said. It was just due to frustration.

"Sorry di, meine kuch bhi bol diya, i am sorry too it was just so reckless of me to say that stuff to you. I am sorry." I walied out like a child.

"Nahi pri tu Mujhe maaf karde, meri vajah se tujhe sacrifice karna padha, us insaan se shadi karni padi jise tu janti bhi nahi thi" di said , her voice slightly cracking up, while i shook my head in "no".

"You are getting it all wrong di, i don't regret marrying him. It's an honour to be his wife, it's an honour to love him and to be loved by him." I said looking up to her, i wiped her tears and she copied me.

"Baba kaise hein ab?" I asked, turning to look at Bhai.

"The doctor did not say anything " Bhai said as he stepped in front of me.

"Hospital chal, Tera hi intezar kar rahe hein baba" Bhai Said keeping a hand over my head.

"Bhai, mein baba se milke wapas Rajasthan chali jaungi, meri flight ki tickets book kar dein aap please" i said as Maan thoughts again struck down my brain, making my heart ache.

"Itne dino baad aayi hai, thode din ruk ja yahi" Bhai said caressing my head.

"Bh-ai, maa-n k-a acci-dent ho gay-a" i said finally disclosing the news to him. Making both di and Bhai shocked.

"Kab hua ye sab? Aur tu mujhe ab bata rahi hai?" Bhai said being shocked.

"Ja-b mei-n yah-a puh-nchi tab hi p-ata ch-ala" i said as my already swollen eyes, started flowing tears of pain and grief once again.

"Ro na meri bacchi, hum tere sath hei" di said embracing me in her warm arms.~~~~~~~~~~We sat in the car, and drove off to the hospital.

AT THE HOSPITALMy knees weakened as i stood in front of baba.

My baba, my strong baba, the one who gave me a new life, was right now on this hospital bed. He looked pale, very pale. My eyes gathered warm tears in them. I hated myself for not being here, when baba needed me.

I gently sat down on the stool placed next to his bed. I took a hold of his right hand. I caressed it ever so gently. I was scared i might hurt him.

"Ba-ba?" I called out for him, he opened his eyes slowly. He looked weak.

"Aagayi meri bacchi?" He asked softening his eyes, he weakly asked me.

"Ye kya ho-gaya baba? Aap to-h mer-e stro-ng ba-ba t-he n-a?" I asked sitting next to him holding his hand.

"Kuch nahi hua gudiya, tere baba abhi bhi strong hai" baba said smiling softly, he was trying to fool me I know.

"Ba-ba do-n't lie to m-e, it's just be-en so-me mon-ths that i w-as away fro-m you, an-d you alre-ady star-ted hid-ing thing-s fro-m me?" I asked with tears making their way out of my eyes.

"Aisa nahi hai" baba said lowly, he seemed running out of energy.

As I was about to say something, the nurse and the doctor came in between inturpting our conversation.

"Mam the patient needs to rest, the meeting hour ends now" the nurse instructed, making me nod.

"And miss, we have to run some medical check-ups on him" the doctor told me and i just nodded.

"It's Mrs. Rajwansh, doctor" i corrected him, he nodded as an answer.

I looked over at baba, and he passed me a weak smile. I planted a kiss over his forehead before leaving the room.

I sighed. Baba gestured me with his hand to smile, and for his sake I did.

I saw Bhai, Maa, di along with Abhishek outside the room, their faces; blank and pale.

I came out of the room, i looked over at them all their faces radiating sadness. It hurts to see all my loved ones bearing any sadness.

I was lost in my thoughts, I was going insane thinking about everything. Maan, baba and both my families.

The doctor came out, and we all rushed to him. I was the first one to ask.

"Doctor is everything alright? Is my baba ok? What do the reports say?" I bombarded him with tons of questions.

"First of all Mrs Rajwansh, relax. Your baba is ok now, and he by god's grace is out of danger." The doctor gave us this news making me take a breath of relief.

"Just make sure that he does not stress out over anything. Stress is like a venom to him at this point. And there are some changes that you have to make in his diet and that's it." The doctor exclaimed looking at all of us.

After telling us this good news, the doctor walked away. That's when Bhaiya said..

"Pri teri flight ka time hogaya bacche" Bhai told me while I nodded. I walked over to maa, i bent down to touch her feet.

"Apna aur baba ka dhyan rakhna, Maa." I told her and as usual no response except for a blank nod.

"Pri sun, koi bhi pareshani ho toh mujhe call kar diyo" Abhishek told me and i smiled being grateful.

"Haan" i replied back to him and he gave me an assuring hug. I bid my goodbye. Later i walked out of the hospital with bhaiya. My mind was all messed up, i tried calling Kiara dharya and Yash but none of them answered their phones. I was going insane every second my heart felt like bursting out with the immense pain I was feeling right now.

~~~~~~~~AT THE AIRPORT~

I got out of the car, Bhai looked at me and nodded his head in an assuring manner.

He came and hugged me gently. I reciprocated back. Though I was not in my complete senses right now, but a hug was all i needed at this point.

"Mera sher baccha" Bhai said and patted my back, he used to say this a lot in my childhood. He parted away.

"Dhayn rakhna apna, mujhe yaad se call kar Dena jab pohonch jayegi toh, idhar ki tension mat Lena, mein sab sambhal lunga. Tu bas Tera aur Abhiman ka dhayan rakh." Bhai said keeping his palm over my head making me nod.

"Chal ab" Bhai said removing his hand from my head. He smiled for the last time looking at me, before i walked away. ~~~~~~~I am settled on my seat. The flight will be taking off anytime now. My worries, that pain, that aching heart of mine, they are not calming. My heart is burning. How can this possibly happen? Why can't I just live in peace? Am i cursed ?

I silently prayed for my both my families. I can not bear to let anything happen to anyone. I can not.

All the time my thoughts kept me awake, but after sometime i found myself drifting off to sleep.~~~~~~So this is it for today!The next update will be on the upcoming Monday! And one thing I wanted to tell you was that I am quite irregular on Wattpad, because of some health problems. And dealing with my personal and professional life along with my health problem is quite difficult but I try to update regularly , but I fail to do so. I am sincerely I am sorry if I ever disappointed you guys! Vote target: 400Take care of yourself until the next update! Stay tuned!
~~~~~~~~

Chapter 31: he did not open his eyes

HIEEEEEEEEEEEEEEE MYYYYYYYYYYYY GOOFBAL-LLLLLLLLSSSS!!!

I have made certain changes in this novel, prisha ki age pehle 19 thi but ab meine 22 kar di hai, legal age for marriage is 21 that is the reason i made this particular change. □

I know I was supposed to update on Monday but, i completed writing it today itself, and I was like post kar hi deti hun. Today's update kinda left me broken, i cried so much that my eyes hurt real bad.

Zyada time na waste karte hue, you can proceed with the story!Hope you will like today's update!~~~~~~~~~~~~~{["Na jaane ye zamaana, Kyun chaahe re mitaana, Kalank nahi ishq hai kaajal piya, Kalank nahi ishq hai kaajal piya" – Kalank]}~~~~~~~~~~~~~PRISHA'S POV I am settled on my seat. The flight will be taking off anytime now. My worries, that pain, that aching heart of mine, they are not calming. My heart is burning. How can this possibly happen? Why can't I just live in peace? Am i cursed ?

I silently prayed for both my families. I cannot bear to let anything happen to anyone. I cannot.

All the time my thoughts kept me awake, but after sometime i found myself drifting off to sleep.~~~~~~~~~~~~~Stepping out of the airport my sight fell on dharya, he seemed to be waiting for me.I walked up to him, he looked at me coming towards him, he smiled a little, a fake smile it seemed.

"Laiye bhabhi-sa ye bag hum le lete hein" he said and i gave it to him. (Now you must be wondering ki prisha ke pass bag toh nahi tha, toh mere bhole goofballs, she must at least have been carrying a bag in which her basic requirements will be right? Like her charger, phone, passport, tissues etc)

"Dharya hospital chalo please" i pleaded him, and he replied with a quick nod.

We both walked towards the car, and settled down real quick. And he drove off to the hospital. All the while my eyes burned with tears brimming out of them. I sat there fidgeting with my mangalsutra. I was scared to death. I was in no state to even think about a life without him. WHY? Why is it happening? Why? My tears flowed free from the edge of my eyes. I probably am looking like a mad woman right now, my puffy red eyes, my messed up hairs, my sindoor smeared up on my forehead, Nevertheless I cared less. My thoughts radiate every worst scenario ever. My heart feared to lose what it loved the most. My eyes craved to see him.

"Plea-se Dha-rya ja-ldi cha-lo" i uttered, my throat hurts, from all the crying and wailing I did.

"Ji bhabhi-sa" he responded back, and speeded up the speed of his car. ~~~~~~~~~~~~~~~I stepped out of the car and as soon as I did, i sprinted inside the hospital, and I was followed by Dharya.

As i walked inside I saw the receptionist, i asked her where Maan was, she told me to wait inside the waiting room, as the doctors were still in, checking Maan. I nodded my head, walking towards the waiting room. Racing against time and battling tears, we arrived at the hospital. The sterile corridors echoed our anxious footsteps. The receptionist confirmed Maan's admission and directed us to the waiting area.

As i entered there, I saw my family as in, mumma, papa ji, Kiara, Yash, and all the other family members. They looked devastated. Just like me. Mumma lifted her head up, as soon as she saw me she got up from her seat, her eyes looked quite similar to mine, puffy and red. I walked towards her more like ran, i landed myself in her embrace. And that was when i broke down completely. The silent tears that were quietly flowing out of my eyes, turned into painfully sorrowful sobs. I screamed, cried and screamed and lost my balance and fell over my knees but mumma didn't leave me. My sobs mixed up with her consolation.

Soon, a doctor approached, his face carrying the weight of difficult news. Pri's heart raced as the doctor explained Maan's critical condition due to the accident. The room became a vacuum, drowning their hope in a sea of despair.

As i absorbed the harsh reality, i felt a surge of determination. "I need to see him," i uttered, my voice trembling but resolute. Mumma supported me, and together we entered the intensive care unit.

Maan lay there, surrounded by machines, his stillness casting a stark contrast to the vibrant spirit i had known. I held his hand, I called out for him, again and again . But he did not open his eyes. He did not look at me. He did not look at his Isha.~~~~~~~~~~~~~~AUTHOR'S POV

Prisha sat in the hospital room, holding her husband Abhiman's hand tightly as tears streamed down her face. She had been sitting there for hours, waiting for him to wake up. The accident had happened so suddenly, and he was now lying on the hospital bed, his body covered in bruises and cuts.

As she sat there, praying for his recovery, a doctor entered the room. Prisha's heart skipped a beat, hoping for some good news. But the look on the doctor's face told her otherwise. He gently placed a hand on her shoulder and said, "I'm sorry, Mrs. Abhiman. Your husband has slipped into a coma."

Prisha felt as if her entire world came crashing down. She couldn't believe what she was hearing. She looked at her Abhiman's peaceful face and then back at the doctor, her eyes filled with tears. "What do you mean he's in a coma? When will he wake up?" she asked, her voice shaking.

The doctor sighed, "I can't say for sure, Mrs. Abhiman. It could be a day, a week, a month, or even years. We just don't know." The doctor exclaimed making her heart sink. She blankly stared at the doctor without uttering anything.

Prisha felt like she was in a daze. Her mind couldn't process the news. Her husband, her soulmate, the love of her life was in a coma, and there was nothing she could do about it. She looked at his peaceful face, and a flood of memories came rushing back. their unexpected wedding, their first kiss, , their silly inside jokes, his teasings. She couldn't imagine a life without him.

Tears rolled down her cheeks like a never-ending stream. She cried and cried, her heart shattering into a million pieces. The reality of the situation hit her hard , her Maan , her husband, the love of her life, her sanity , could be gone forever, or he could wake up and have no recollection of their life together. Either way, it felt like a nightmare.

Prisha's world shattered at that moment. She couldn't believe what she was hearing. Her Maan, the love of her life, the one person who had always been her rock, was now lying in a coma. She felt her chest constrict, her breathing became labored, and the tears that she had been holding back came pouring out.

She broke down, crying and holding onto her Abhiman's hand as if her life depended on it.

The doctor and Abhiman's mother tried to comfort her, explaining that coma patients often wake up, but Prisha couldn't hear anything beyond the fact that her husband was in danger. She felt like she was in a nightmare and couldn't wake up. She wanted to shake Abhiman and make him open his eyes, make him come back to her.

As the doctor and Abhiman's mother left the room, giving her some privacy. Prisha couldn't stop her sobs. She cried and cried, her mind unable to process the thought of not having her Maan by her side. She felt lost, alone, and scared. Her mind was flooded with memories of their happy moments together, making the current reality even harder to bear.

Prisha sat in the hospital room, her hand tightly gripping Abhiman's hand. Tears streamed down her face as she watched her love, lying still on the bed, his face pale and bruised from the accident. It felt like a nightmare, a cruel joke. Just some days ago, they were happy and laughing, dreaming of their future together. And now, here she was, sitting in the hospital, holding on to her Maan's hand for dear life, praying for a miracle.

Prisha's heart felt like it stopped beating. She couldn't believe what she was hearing. This couldn't be happening. She looked at Abhiman's still form, praying that he would wake up and prove the doctor wrong. Prisha's heart broke. She felt like a part of her was missing, that she would never be whole again. She prayed to every god she knew, promising anything and everything if only her husband would wake up. But did he wake up? No.

She sat there for what felt like hours, holding onto the love of her life, praying for him to wake up. The doctor's words echoed in her head. " It could be a day, a week, a month, or even years. We just can't say for sure."

Prisha's world crumbled around her as the reality of the situation sank in. She clutched onto Abhiman's limp hand, her tears falling on his skin. She couldn't bear the thought of her Maan lying here, unaware of the world around him.~~~~~~~The next few days were a blur for Prisha. She refused to leave Abhiman's side, ignoring her own basic needs. When she wasn't talking to him, she was staring at him, hoping for some sign of life. She couldn't wrap her head around the fact that her husband was in a coma, and there was nothing she could do to bring him back.

The doctors had recommended therapy for Prisha, seeing her deteriorating mental state. But she refused to leave her husband's side, insisting that she was fine. But deep down, Prisha was a mess. She felt like she was drowning in a sea of hopelessness and despair.

As the days turned into weeks, and then into months, Prisha's mental state worsened. It became harder for her to hold on to hope, and she couldn't help but wonder if Abhiman would ever wake up. She spent every waking moment by his side, whispering words of love and encouragement, hoping that he could somehow hear her.~~~~~~~~~~~~~There was this one day she sat by his side, she reached for his hand and noticed that his fingers slightly twitched. Prisha's heart skipped a beat, and she leaned in closer, her hopes rising. Abhiman's eyes fluttered open, and Prisha's heart leaped with joy. But as she looked into his eyes, she noticed that they were empty and lifeless.

It was then that Prisha realized that her Maan was still in a coma. He had just moved slightly due to a reflex, but there was no sign of consciousness. Prisha's heart shattered into a million pieces, and she broke down in sobs.

She couldn't take it anymore. The uncertainty, the hopelessness, it was all too much. Prisha's mental state finally broke, and she suffered a full-blown breakdown. The doctors had to sedate her and put her in a separate room to calm her down.

As she lay in the hospital bed, her tears drying on her cheeks, Prisha couldn't help but wonder if she would ever be able to pick up the pieces of her shattered life. She didn't know how much longer she could take the pain and the uncertainty.

But even in her darkest moments, Prisha refused to give up on her husband. She held on to the little hope she had left, praying for a miracle. Because to her, Abhiman was worth it. He was the love of her life, and she would do anything to bring him back.

There was no sign of Abhiman waking up, Prisha felt her world crumbling around her. She tried to remain strong for her husband, but inside, she was falling apart.

The hospital became her second home, and the nurses became her family. They would often find her holding on to Abhiman's hand, tears streaming down her face, as she whispered words of love and hope to him. They could see the love and pain in her eyes, and they couldn't help but feel for her.

Rishabh, Sneha, her baba, Abhishek and her maa are also in Rajasthan, they came the next moment when they heard about the situation. In-laws were always there offering their love and support. Dharya, Yash and Kiara often tried to console her, crack silly jokes to make her laugh But nothing could ease the pain of seeing her Maan in that state, and not knowing if he would ever wake up.

In the midst of all this, Prisha couldn't help but feel guilty. She blamed herself for not being able to protect Abhiman, for not being able to prevent the accident. She felt like she had let him down, and she didn't know if she could live with that guilt. If she could have informed him before going to Delhi, this would not have happened.

But amidst all the despair, Prisha held on to hope. She believed that their love was strong enough to bring Abhiman back to her. She refused to give up, and every day, she would pray for a miracle.

Even in her darkest moments, one thought kept her going , the thought of Abhiman waking up and them being together again. She would do anything to make that dream a reality.

She closed her eyes and let out a prayer, hoping that this would be the day her husband would wake up. She prayed for a miracle, a second chance, and a happily ever after. And with that thought in her heart, Prisha held on to hope and waited for her Maan to return to her. ~~~~~~~~~~~~~~~That's it for today! Agala chapter jaise hi likh ke ho Jayega I'll post it!Stay tuned!Vote target 500!~~~~~~~~~~~~~~~

Chapter 32: Prank

~ ~~~~~~{Aavan javan te main yaara nu manavan, Enna sona, enna sona" – Enna Sona (OK Jaanu)}~~~~~~~AUTHOR'S POV As days passed, there was no improvement in Abhiman's condition. The doctors were not able to give any assurance about his recovery. Prisha's hope and faith started to fade, and she was on the verge of losing all hope.

Prisha was shattered. Her world had come crashing down. She couldn't bear to see Abhiman in that state, lying lifeless on the hospital bed. Every day, she would sit by his side, holding his hand and praying for his recovery. She would talk to him, hoping that he could hear her and would wake up.

But as days passed, there was no improvement in Abhiman's condition. The doctors were not able to give any assurance about his recovery. Prisha's hope and faith started to fade, and she was on the verge of losing all hope.

Today was no different, she was sitting by Abhiman's side, she broke down and started crying uncontrollably. She begged him to wake up, to fight for their love, for their life together. She told him how much she needed him, how much she loved him. She refused to give up on him, no matter what.

As if in response to her cries, Abhiman's hand twitched, Prisha couldn't believe her eyes. Her prayers had been answered. She couldn't believe it and immediately went to call the doctor.

"Doc-tor I-I-I-----voh Maa-n, he mov-ed his han-ds" prisha shuttered, her eyes welled up with tears of happiness, the doctor passed a smile towards her.

"Mrs. Abhiman, let us first go and examine him, because we still don't know if that was just a reflex or he really is responding now" the doctor explained when she nodded her head repeatedly.

The nurse and the doctors along with prisha moved towards Abhiman's ward.

As the doctor examined him, Abhiman slowly opened his eyes. Prisha's heart skipped a beat as she saw her Maan looking at her with confusion in his eyes. Her heart ached as she looked at the confusion filled in his eyes.

"Mr. Abhiman, can you hear me?" The doctor asked, examining him.

"Yes" Abhiman replied with a quick nod.

"Ohk, so do you remember anything regarding this accident?" The doctor inquired, Abhiman shook his head.

"I do not" Abhiman answered making prisha's heart race fast.

"Alright, do you remember about your family? Do you remember her?" The doctor said pointing prisha out. Prisha's heart thumped faster, as Abhiman turned his gaze to look at her.

"I don't remember her" Said Abhiman, breaking the left over pieces of her heart, her eyes turned red, as tears started gathering in her eyes.

"Doctor, can you please give me a minute, alone with my husband?" Prisha said almost pleading, looking at her vulnerable state the doctor nodded her head, gesturing the nurses to step out along with him.

Prisha started walking towards Abhiman, her eyes tearing up already.

She knelt down beside his bed, searched out for his hand, she held his hand making him look at her, he looked at her clearly confused, making her heart shatter.

"Y-ou don't remember me?" She asked him, her voice already shaking.

"Who are you?" He asked back instead of replying, making her hopes die down her heart. Her tears flowed free from her eyes.

She got up from her knees she sat beside the little space beside him, she cupped his cheeks, her tears flowed like a never ending river.

"Aapko hum yaad nahi?" She uttered.

"Nahi" he spoke, making her remove her hands off his cheeks. She shook her head not believing it.

Prisha was taken aback by this. She couldn't believe that the man she loved with all her heart didn't remember her. She tried to explain to him who she was, but he just couldn't remember anything about their life together.

Heartbroken and shattered, Prisha couldn't hold back her tears. She cried uncontrollably as she realized that the man she loved was now a stranger to her. She couldn't understand how he could forget all the memories they had created together, the love they had shared, and the promises they had made to each other.

"KAISE HUM AAPKO YAAD NAHI? HUH? PYAAR KA VADA KARTE THE NAA AAP? KAHA GAYA AAPKA PYAR? ITNA KACCHA AUR KAMZOR THA AAPKA PYAR? KAISE NAHI

YAAD AAPKO? BATAIYE?!? HUME NAHI PATA HUME HAMARE MAAN VAPAS CHAHIYE!" she yelled at him, while gripping onto the collar of his hospital uniform.

She scooted closer to him, hugging him tightly. She was not ready to let go of him. She was not. Not now, not in this universe. She walied like a child trying to digest what she just heard.

"Ishq hei Hume aapse, mohabbat, junoon, dil-lagi, ulfat, pyar. Jo aap kehna chahe, I love you! I love you! Your presence makes me feel alive, and I can't explain it. It's more than just love, it's beyond love. it's like you make my heart, body, and mind react in a way that's hard to put into words. Your affection filled eyes, your soothing touch, your voice , your love, your entire being, they made me fall insanely in love with you. It's not just love, it's my heart, it's your heart, it's our heart. It's our little universe. I'm in love with you, Abhiman Singh Rajvansh. Can't you feel it? Tell me you can please" she cried in his arms, she felt her world stop. She refused to believe any of it. Her Maan can not do this to her. She doesn't believe it. Any. Of. It.

"I can" Abhiman said wrapping his arms around her. Her eyes that seemed to flow tears in the form of rivers, had stopped abruptly. She felt all that again.

She lifted her blood shot eyes up, to look at him. Her eyes, tried to find her Abhiman back. And she did. Her Maan. Only hers.

WAIT- was he pulling out a prank right now? She realised it, that he was faking his memory loss.

She lightly slapped him, accross his face. How could he do this! He can't be real for pulling out this stunt. In the reflex his face tilted slightly. Making her widen her eyes. She realised what she did. She immediately placed her hands where she just slapped him, " Sorryyyyy" she said as she caressed that spot gently. Her eyes filled with tears.

"Apni pasandida aurat se thappad khane mein sharam kis baat ki?" He said grinning, at the fact he got to feel her touch, after what seems like eternity.

"Agar Hume pata hota ki aap itne pyar se aapki mohabbat ka izhar karengi, toh hum sau aur accidents karwane ko tyar hein" he spoke but prisha shushed him while keeping her index finger on his lips. She shook her head indicating him not to continue further.

"Kyun kiya aapne esa?" She asked hiccuping, when he lifted his hand that had, saline attached to it, he caressed her jaw.

"Aapko ye ehsaas dilane ke liye, ki aap humse pyar karti hein" he said as he continued Caressing her jaw.

"Hum dar Gaye the, Hume laga aap hume bhul gaye" she spoke as her eyes again spilled tears, it broke his heart to see her in this condition.

"Hum ese hi nahi aapko humari Jaan kehte hein, jaan hein aap humari, jaan basti hein humari aapme. Pehchan hein aap humari, bhala koi apni pe-hchan bhul sakta hai? Agar hum aapko bhul gaye matlab humne hamesha astitva kho diya" He spoke looking into her eyes, he felt at peace. Looking at her, itself healed him.

"Mohabaat hogayi hai Hume aapse." Prisha spoke drowning herself in his eyes.

If i knew that my accident would get her to confess her feelings, i would have had a accident way before.

"Jante hein Hume, 30. 1. 24. " his eyes gazed at her teary ones. I widened my eyes, as because this was the actually the date i realised my feelings for him.

"KAISE?" She nearly screamed. Making him chuckle out loud.

"Jab Aap aapke pyar ka izhar kar, rahi thi ye sochkar ke hum so rahe the, what was it again?"He looked so peaceful while sleeping, he's just so pure and selfless isn't he? He cares for me like the way i care for my loved ones, he loves me like the way fictional men love their female leads and he looks at me like I am some kind of a gem. But in reality he's the real gem, a rare one, the one only I can have.", " He mimicked her. Making her ears turn red out of embarrassment.

"Soye nahi the aap us samay?" Prisha questioned.

"Aap agar ese baatein humare sone ke baad karengi, toh aapko kya lagta hei hum soyenge, ?aap agar esi baatein karenge toh Puri raat haste haste jagne ko tyaar hein" he spoke making her giggle.

"Ek baat kahen?" Abhiman asked, while prisha hummed still looking into his eyes.

"Hume aapse pagalo wali mohabbat hein, jaan de sakte hein hum aapke liye, aap kahe toh aapke liye jaan le bhi sakte hein." Abhiman exclaimed while he wiped her tears off.

He as usual kissed her tears making her giggle. They both sat there, talking about stuffs, giggling, and laughing. Until the doctor came and told that it's time for Abhiman to rest.

At first he showed tantrums, but after one glare from Prisha he gave up.

Prisha walked out of there, calling both her family to inform this good news.~~~~~~~~~Heart attack diya Abhiman ne prank karke? Aur Han ab tum sab soch rahe honge ki in dono ki family kaha hai, toh to clarify, mereko ye chapter sirf indono ke liye banana tha, isliye unka part add nahi Kiya, ye Maan lo ki voh Ghar pe the.So finally, ab sab happy happy?That's it for today!Ab mein 1-2 hafte baad dalungi update, (padhai is killing me, but nevermind)Untill then take care of yourself!Vote target: 600~~~~~~~~~

Chapter 33: Happiness

Ohk first all showwyyyyyy itni late update ke liye, my examinations are going on. Will try to update as soon as I get free.! Love you all!!~your author~~~~~~~~~~~~("Kisi ki muskurahaton pe ho nisar, kisi ka dard mil sake to le udhar" – Anari)~~~~~~~~~~~~Days passed by and Abhiman showed signs of improvement. But he was still too weak to eat solid food. The doctors advised Prisha to feed Abhiman liquid food.

Abhiman being Abhiman threw tantrums to eat hospital cooked meals, that was when prisha took the matters in her own hands. She herself cooked his meals, it used to be mostly porridge, daal chawal, khichdi, soup, mashed potatoes and many other stuff.

She was as usual feeding him with her hands, while he was eating it like a happy child. He wanted nothing more than this, he wanted to just sit and admire her forever. Even forever seems less to him.

"Hum kabse kuch keh rahe hein aapse, aapka dhyan kaha hein?" Prisha asked pulling him out of his thoughts.

"Hum sun rahe hein, aap bolti jayein" Abhiman said making her raise eyebrows.

"Accha ji? Chalen batayen hum kya bol rahe the?" She asked him, not believing that he was paying any head to her words.

"Aap hume yeh keh rahi thi, ki hume aaram karna chahiye, hume apna khayal rakhna chahiye." He told her, while she just nodded at him, feeding him another morsel.

"Can we please go back home?" Abhiman's rant started, it's nothing new. He's been saying this for the past few days. Prisha sighed.

"Kya hogaya hai aapko Maan? Kesi behki behki baatein kar rahen hai aap?" Prisha said shaking her head while stuffing morsels full of daal chawal in his mouth.

He chewed it before saying "Hume aapse kuch zyada hi pyar hogaya hai, behek toh hum use din Gaye the jis din hum aapke pyar mein gir gaye the"

"Chup rahiye bilkul. Pata bhi hai hum kitne daar Gaye the aapke us prank ki vajah se? Hume laga tha ki aap hume bhul gaye" prisha said as she tilted her face sideways, while folding her hands over her chest.

"Your name, Your voice, your love, your fragrance, your touch, everything about you, and especially you. All of it is engraved within me. I can even recognise you from your heartbeat. Nobody can make it fade. Not you. Not me." Abhiman said as he kept his index finger on her chin, tilting it in his direction.

"Hufff kaha se utha ke laate hein ye romantic lines aap? Aapse hum nahi jeet sakte, na baaton mein na hi kisi aur cheez mein, after all my husband is an all rounder, no?" Prisha said chuckling, while smiling cutely.

"If you want I'd never be right. You would win every argument. Every game, you would win everything, including my heart. As it should be." Abhiman said opening his mouth, taking in another morsel full of food.

"Aishhh khana khaye chup chap" prisha said as he chuckled softly at her innocence.

Prisha took it upon herself to take care of Abhiman. She made sure that he was comfortable and had all the necessary things by his side. She would sit by his bed every day, feeding him daal chawal with her own hands. Seeing her love and dedication, Abhiman's condition started to improve rapidly.

Prisha never left his side, not even for a second. She knew that she was his strength and her love for him would help him recover faster.

Abhiman was done eating his food. And now it was the last morsel he was about to consume, prisha forwarded a mouthful of morsels. He took it in his mouth and bit on her fingers lightly, making her wince a little. She looked at him wide eyed while he just innocently passed her a small smile.

"Ye kya tha Maan? Bilkul doggy ki tarah Katta hai aapne, janwar Bane ka shauk Chad Gaya hai kya aapko?" Prisha said fake glaring at him, while he just passed her a slay smirk.

"Bhaw bhaw" he fake barked making her eyes go wide.

"Aapka accident ke baad dimag pura kharab hogaya hai Maan, sharam nahi aati ese biwi ke sath flirt karte hue?" Prisha said, her mouth wide open.

"Sharam ka toh pata nahi par jab bhi aap esi maasoomiyat bhari baate karti hein, toh aapko humare bacchon ki maa banane ki feeling zarur aati hei" Abhiman stated shamelessly, making prisha's face turn red due to shyness.

Abhiman being the shameless person he is, pulled her closer by keeping his hand on the nape of her back, making her gasp.

"Chore hume, koi aa jayega" Prisha said slightly pushing him away, meanwhile he tightened his hold around her.

"Koi nahi aayega" Abhiman assured her, making her shake her head, Abhiman leaned in, he was about to join his lips with her Petal ones, but Prisha pushed him, when she heard the clearing of throat.

Abhiman and prisha looked up, only to find the nurse standing there Blushing, while standing with her head hung low.

"Si-r vo actua-lly, aap-ki fam-ily yah-a aa-yi hai. Aa-pse mil-ne" she shuttered, making Prisha widen her eyes.

"You can go, tell them to come inside" Abhiman uttered in his cold tone.

She nodded her head and left after bowing her head.

One by one everybody came, blessed him. And not to forget how mumma scolded him for being a reckless fellow and driving like a drunkard.

Abhiman was sipping on his juice that prisha brought, that was when he heard his dadi say

"Jaldi se Ghar aaja beta, hume bhi Marne se pehle humare pota poti ka chehara dekhna hai" dadi stated making him choke on his juice, he coughed hard, while prisha patted his back.

"Seriously dadi? I am literally on a hospital bed right now" Abhiman said, recovering from his deadly cough.

"Heyyy bhagwan matlab mein chacha nahi banunga? Exactly lagi kaha aapko?!?" Yash yelled, making everyone burst out in laughter.

"Yash fvcking Rajwansh shut the damn up" Abhiman glared at Yash.

"Isko for real mental hospital mein chor ke aana chahiye" Dharya said sarcastically.

"Miracle, janwaro jaisi baat karne laga hai ye gadha, Tujhko toh zoo mein se bahar kon nikala?" Yash scoffed as he stated this.

"Tujhe jesa uncultured bandar Jo paal rakha hai, tere liye hi janwaro wali bhasha sikhi, Varna tereko kon samajhta?" Dharya replied back in a very slay tone.

"Tum logo ne fukk ke Rakhi hai?" Abhiman finally spoke out, being done with their conversation.

"Kaise apman janik baatein kare ho sab, eww" Kiara said making a disgusting face.

"Chill kar Teri baat nahi hori" Yash said, frustratedly, prisha and Abhiman muffed their laughter.

"Us chill ki pill bana, aur tu hi kha le" Kiara said pointing her finger at Yash, making everyone burst out laughing.

"Ab Teri jaise chapri se suggestions lun?" Yash scoffed.

"Mere itne standards nahi gir ve hein ki tujh jaise saarfire ko apne kimti suggestions dun" Kiara said flipping her hairs.

"Baal Tut jayenge, mat kar" dharya said, making her gape at his words, both Yash and Dharya hi-fied.

"Sab ke sab janwar ho" Abhiman's mother said shaking her head looking at the drama unfolding and they all looked at her making innocent faces.

"Meri laadoo ko chor ke tum sab gadhe ho" Abhiman's mother said walking towards prisha and planting a small kiss on her forehead, making her giggle.

"Maa haad hai, aapka beta bimar pada hai aur aap apni bahu ko pyar kar rahi ho? Not fair yarr" Abhiman said making a fake sulky face.

"Han jaise meri Bahu hi thi vo Jo us raat sharabiyo ki tarah car chala Rahi thi? Haina?" Abhiman's mother said with her voice filled with sweet sarcasm. Meanwhile Abhiman shook his head.

He looked at his family who were laughing happily, he would want this to never end. He smiled looking at his family. It was all of them being happy. He can't be more grateful.~~~~~~~~~~~~~~~Chotu sa tha ik ik but Aaj ke liye itna hi!Vote target 700 !Byeeeyeyeyeyeyeyeyeyeyeyeyeyeyeiiiiiiiiiiiii-iiiiiiiiiiii~~~~~~~~~~~~~~

chapter 34 : EXYZ

~~~~~~~~~~~~~~Author aaj phir trauma degiiiiiiiiiiiiiSorry in advance goofballs ~~~~~~~~~~~~~{"Oh Jinke Liye Hum Rotey Hain, Wo Kisi Aur Ki Baahon Mein Sotey Hain" – Jinke Liye (Neha Kakkar)}~~~~~~~~~~~~~AUTHOR'S POV

It's been a week since Abhiman has been discharged from the hospital, Prisha took really good care of him, that helped him recover fast.

As now Abhiman was all fine, the trio of Kiara, Yash and dharya decided to have some fun.

Tonight, Yash and Kiara had insisted that they all go out and have some fun. Despite their initial reservations, Prisha and Abhiman had agreed to join them. Little did they know that this night would turn out to be quite eventful.

"All ready?" Abhiman asked looking at prisha fixing her dress.

"Yess" prisha passed him a sweet shy smile.

He held out his hand indicating prisha to hold it, which she gladly did. They both smiled at each other before walking downstairs.
~~~~~~~~~~~~~~

There stood the three of the monkeys. The three of them looked at the couple stepping down with awe.

"Hayeee kitne pyare lag rahe ho aap dono" Kiara said keeping a hand over her chest.

"Bhai-sa ka toh pata nahi lekin meri bhabhi-sa toh ekdum pari jaisi lag rahi hein, hayeeeeee" Yash exclaimed, grinning widely.

"Mukka mar ke dant Tod Dene hai meine tere, battisi dikhana band kar" Abhiman said glaring at him.

"Pehli baar kuch sahi bola hai is bandar ne" Dharya said agreeing with Yash.

"Mein bandar? Toh Tu gian" Yash retorted back.

"Aur tu suneo" Dharya said sarcastically.

"Bas bas, hum sabhi hi pyare lag rahe hein" prisha said dissming their fight.

"Chale phir?" Kiara said as everyone nodded.

~~~~~~~~

Yash had booked a VIP table at one of the most exclusive clubs in town. As they made their way inside, they were greeted with loud music, flashing lights and the smell of alcohol. The place was buzzing with energy and the dance floor was packed with people.

Aadvik and lakshay were invited too, they never really had a chance to meet prisha and they wanted to meet her, so Abhiman decided to tag them along with all of them.

The group settled at their table and ordered some drinks. Abhiman, being a billionaire, didn't hesitate to splurge on the most expensive bottle of champagne for everyone to enjoy. Prisha, on the other hand, was feeling
~~~~~~~~

a little out of place. She wasn't used to the party scene and felt a bit uncomfortable.

"Jaana? Are you comfortable?" Abhiman asked sensing her discomfort. Prisha passed a small smile at him and nodded her head.

Dharya got up and gestured everybody to get on the dance floor, Abhiman as usual refused, Kiara somehow managed to convince prisha, currently She was dancing with Yash and Kiara, while Abhiman watched them with a smile on his face. She was having the time of her life.

Prisha saw him sitting there sipping onto his drink, not liking the Idea of him consuming alcohol Prisha went towards him and grabbed his hand, pulling him towards the dance floor.

Abhiman couldn't resist her infectious energy and went along with her. They danced together, laughing and spinning around. But as they danced, Prisha stumbled and fell, causing Abhiman to catch her in his arms.

"Ouchh" prisha hissed in pain, making Abhiman widened his eyes.

"Jaan? You ok?" Abhiman immediately asked with his voice laced with concern.

"Jii" prisha meekly nodded.

"Not at all" he said as He quickly picked her up and carried her back to their table. Yash and Kiara dharya and the two of his best friends were too busy dancing to notice and Abhiman didn't want to ruin their fun.

"Wait for me here, I'll go get you something to drink" Abhiman said and Prisha nodded.~~~~~~ABHIMAN'S POV

I made my way towards the soft drink section, as I walked I bumped into someone. Whoever the person was had a drink in their hands that just got spilled over my suit. I looked up with rage filled inside of my eyes, but however seeing the person left me in shock.

It was my ex. Himani.

She gazed into my eyes, making me break the eye contact. I hate her.

"Abhi?" She muttered out my name making me look at her with disgust. The audacity of her to call me by my nickname is insane.

"It's Abhiman. Singh.Rajwansh. for you" i spoke out looking at her dead in the eye. The urge to kill her is getting real right now.

"Baby- i cut her off in between "don't call me by that name, i swear I won't hesitate chopping your tongue off your mouth, right here, right now, right at this point." I said while my jaw tightened, my eyes were red.

"Let's talk it out, you loved me, i loved you. And I am sure you are still not over me."

"You can go and die for all i care, high of you to think that I cannot get over a cheater like you" Abhiman said through gritted teeth. He couldn't believe she had the audacity to show up unannounced after what she did to him.

he was fuming. He couldn't believe that she had the audacity to come back into his life. The memories of their relationship started flooding back into his mind, and he was filled with anger and disgust. How could she just show up like this after all these years?--FLASHBACK-Abhiman and Himani were in college, they both were a happy couple. And today was the day he was finally gonna confess his love to her. Abhiman, Aadvik and lakshay prepared all the necessary stuff.

Now it was the time, Abhiman dialled Himani's number, she did not pick it up. Unusual of her. He called her numerous times but there was no response. He became worried and decided to go to her apartment, he was stunned to find her sleeping with another man, whom she used to call her "best friend". He was devastated, that day, he kept his self respect aside and begged her to come with him, saying he will forget whatever happened today but she did not hesitate while rejecting him. He became a very cold hearted person, he stopped believing in love and slowly moved on from her, he was a very practical person, and this is what helped him move on.

FLASHBACK ENDS--"You have some nerve showing your face to me," he spat at her.

Himani looked shocked and taken aback. "Abhiman, please listen to me. I know I hurt you, but I was young and dumb back then. I've changed now and I just want to apologize and make things right."

Abhiman's grip on his phone tightened that he was holding in his hands as he heard her words. He couldn't believe that she was trying to justify her actions. "Do you even realize how much you hurt me? How much you shattered me when I found out about your affair? And now you have the audacity to come back and apologize? I don't want your apologies, Himani. I don't want any part of you in my life."

Himani's face fell, and she started tearing up. "Please, Abhiman. I still love you. I made a huge mistake and I regret it every day. Please give me a chance to make things right."

Abhiman couldn't believe what he was hearing. She still loved him? After all this time? He scoffed at her. "You don't love me, Himani. You just realized that you couldn't find anyone better than me. Well, guess what? It's too late. I've moved on."

Just then, he heard a soft sob behind him. He turned around to see his wife, his Isha , standing there with tears streaming down her face. "Maan, is t-his true? D-o y-ou lov-e he-r? A-re you goi-ng to leav-e m-e?" Prisha said, her words breaking down in between.

Abhiman was taken aback by the sight of her crying. He rushed towards her and tried to explain the situation, but she wouldn't listen. "Isha, please listen to me. She's my ex-girlfriend. She cheated on me and I broke up with her. I would never leave you like that."

She did not listen to anything instead She ran away from there crying, leaving Abhiman feeling guilty and angry at the same time.

He turned towards Himani, who was looking at them with a smug smile. "See? I told you, Abhi. You still love me. You can't let go of me. And about that bivth wife of yours? I am better than her, in every way, you know what i mean right?"

Abhiman's anger got the best of him and he grabbed Himani by the arm. "You are a freaking cheater, my wife, my queen, my love, my Isha is better than you in every aspect . Leave, Himani. I don't want to see your face ever again. And if you ever try to come near Prisha again, I will make sure you regret it. And I am sure you know what I mean"

With that, he stormed away, leaving Himani standing there with a shocked expression. Abhiman couldn't believe that she had the nerve to come back into his life and try to ruin his marriage. He was determined to not let her come between him and Prisha ever again.

Chapter 35: Prove it

~ ~~~~~~This chapter will content mature content ahead. Proceed only if you are comfortable.~~~~~~~{(Labon ko labon se churaalo, Kya ho tum, mjhe ab btaao) -laabon ko}~~~~~~~PRISHA'S POV

As I was sitting there waiting for Maan, it's been almost 15 mins since he has gone, being worried my gaze wandered here and there, i saw lakshay bhaiya coming towards me. I gave him a smile.

"Heyyy bhabhi! Aap idhar? Aap dance floor pe the na? Phir idhar kaise aagaye?" Lakshay bhaiya spoke.

"Voh hum girne wali thi, phir Maan ne bacha liya, humne bola ki I am alright but he did not listen and brought me here" i told him while he chuckled.

"Phir Abhiman kaha gaya?" Lakshay bhaiya asked.

"Humare liye soft drink lene Gaye hein" I spoke softly, as my gaze wandered once again, they landed on Maan, he was talking with a girl. She was heavenly beautiful. She was talking with him, it somehow made my heart clench.

"Aap janti hai use bhabhi?" Lakshay bhaiya spoke.

"Nahi" i said my gaze is still on them.

"Aapko haq hai janne ka, voh ex hai Abhiman ki" bhaiya spoke as my head instantly turned towards bhaiya.

"K-ya" i uttered not believing what he just said.

"Jii" lakshay bhaiya nodded while sipping onto his drink.

"Can you order me one of these drinks?" I said out of the blue, lakshay bhaiya chocked on his drink.

"Bhabhi it's alcohol, not a soft drink"Bhaiya exclaimed but I was too stubborn to listen to him, at last he gave up and ordered me the alcoholic drink.

I chugged onto 3 of the shots, lakshay bhaiya looked at me wide eyed.

"Bhabhi that's too much for you, Abhiman is gonna kill me" bhaiya said.

"Bhaiya I'll be back" i said as i got up, with my tipsy steps I walked near Maan, the music was now at its lowest, i could hear them speak very clearly.

Tears streamed down my throat, my throat ached badly, wanting to release a sob, and i let our a soft sob.

He turned around to see me standing there with tears streaming down my face. "Maan, is t-his true? D-o y-ou lov-e he-r? A-re you goi-ng to leav-e m-e?" I said, my words breaking down in between.

Abhiman was taken aback by the sight of me crying. He rushed towards me and tried to explain the situation, but i wouldn't listen. "Isha, please listen to me. She's my ex-girlfriend. She cheated on me and I broke up with her. I would never leave you like that."

I did not listen to anything instead i ran away from there crying, leaving Abhiman feeling guilty and angry at the same time.

AUTHOR'S POV

She ran away, rushing to somewhere. She stopped near the washroom and sat down on the floor, tears made their way out of her eyes. She hated herself for being this weak.

But as she sat down, she could feel the alcohol hitting her hard, she felt Someone keeping a hand over her shoulder she recognised the touch. and she couldn't control the words that were spilling out of her mouth.

"Why are you even with me, Abhiman?" she slurred, tears welling up in her eyes. "I can never compete with someone like her. Someone who is beautiful, successful, and obviously still has a hold on you."

Abhiman's expression turned from concern to anger as he looked at his wife. "Don't you ever say that, Prisha. You are the most beautiful, intelligent, and amazing woman I have ever met. And I love you. No one else holds a candle to you."

"Then why did you not tell me about your past? It was not like i would not trust you!" She yelled at him through her tears.

"Was it necessary jaan? I love you and you know it" Maan spoke and I lost the last bit of it.

"You love me? Prove it to me then" Prisha said her eyes locking up with his.

"Meri jaan you are drunk right now, let's go home we will talk it out tomorrow ok?" Abhiman said as He could smell the alcohol on her breath and knew that she was drunk.

"I said prove it to me Maan" Prisha stubbornly said, Abhiman chuckled, Abhiman was taken aback by her sudden outburst, but he could understand where she was coming from. He knew that she needed reassurance, and he was ready to give it to her.

"You won't be able to stand me showing my love to you" Abhiman said as a small smile played on his face.

"I want to know. I really do." Prisha spoke.

Warning : mature content ahead (sensitive people can skip)

Without a word, Abhiman picked her up. He booked a room and took her inside. Prisha was a bit confused and overwhelmed by Abhiman's actions, but she trusted him and went along with it. Once inside the room, Abhiman locked the door behind them and turned to Prisha. He could see the doubt and fear in her eyes, and he knew that he had to do something to make her feel secure again.

Abhiman placed prisha on the soft mattress, He leaned in, With aching need, he lifted prisha into his arms, his lips never leaving hers. He carried her towards the bed, their bodies pressed tightly together as he laid her down gently on the soft white sheets. Prisha gazed up at him, her eyes full of longing and desire. his lips meeting prisha's, who closed her eyes, sensing his gentle touch. The kiss deepened, their connection growing stronger. Prisha's arms encircled Abhiman's neck, while he held her, creating a moment where both were immersed in the kiss. In that instant, prisha understood she couldn't maintain the distance any longer surrendering to Abhiman had become inevitable, a choice neither of them could resist or control.

"Do you still want me to prove it to you?" Abhiman asked not sure if he should continue.

"Read my eyes Maan, they want you. So does every inch of me" Prisha said her eyes telling him the love she has for him.

Their eyes met with a mix of desire and passion. The room was filled with soft music, adding to the romantic atmosphere. She leaned in to kiss him, feeling his warmth against her lips. He slowly traced his hands down her back, sending shivers down her spine.

As their kisses grew more intense, she ran her hands through his hair, pulling him closer. He softly caressed her face, savoring the taste of her lips. The moon outside was now fully visible, casting a warm glow over their bodies.

"Meri jaan you still have a chance, stop me while you can" Abhiman spoke as he took deep breaths to calm himself down.

"I want to know how it feels to be owned by Abhiman Singh Rajwansh. Make me yours" prisha said and that was the permission he needed. He kissed her forehead and lowered his face kissing her eyes, her nose, her lips and finally her chin and lastly the Crook of her neck.

Abhiman gently pulled down the straps of prisha's outfit, bringing them closer. Before long, they both ended up on the bed, covered in sheets, with their clothes scattered around the room.

Their hands roamed each other's bodies, exploring and discovering every inch. As they removed each other's clothes, the room was filled with the sound of their heavy breathing and moans.

The moon was peeking through the curtains, casting a silvery glow over the room and highlighting the elegant decor.

Without a word, Abhiman once again captured her lips in a fiery kiss, his hands lightly caressing her cheeks. Prisha yielded to his touch, her body melting against his as their tongues danced in a passionate embrace. their connection grew stronger with each passing moment. Now, in this moonlit room, they were finally alone and ready to surrender to each other.

Abhiman's hands roamed over prisha's body, his touch igniting a fire within her. She moaned softly, her body arching towards him as he gently sucked on her neck. The sensation sent waves of pleasure coursing through her body, causing her to grip onto him even tighter. She could feel the desire burning within her, her body begging for more.

Abhiman's hands roamed over her body, gently teasing and exploring every inch of her. Prisha's skin was soft and warm under his touch, and he couldn't resist trailing his lips down her neck, kissing and nipping at her sensitive skin. Prisha's breathing became shallow as she surrendered herself to the pleasure, her body trembling with every touch.

Abhiman traced his fingers down Prisha's body, feeling every curve and dip of her soft skin. She responded eagerly to his touch, her moans of pleasure filling the room. As he kissed her deeply, his hands roamed freely, igniting every nerve in her body.

He moved down to her neck and started to suck on her delicate skin, causing Prisha to let out a soft cry. She had never felt such intense pleasure from a kiss before. Her body arched in response to the pleasure, surrendering herself completely to him. Abhiman sucked on her neck, eliciting moans of pleasure from Prisha.

But then, his lips moved to a particular spot on her spine, a scar that had always made Prisha feel insecure. The scar that monster gave her. She tensed up, expecting him to pull away or make a comment. But to her surprise, he continued to kiss the scar, with the same tenderness as before.

"Don't kiss me over my scar Maan, you will get yourself dirty" prisha spoke as tears slipped off her eyes.

"If kissing over this scar of yours makes me dirty, i would prefer to be dirty, believe me I would never want to be cleaned." Abhiman spoke taking her insecurities away from her, And as he did, he whispered sweet words to her, telling her how beautiful she was, how perfect she was to him.

Prisha felt a wave of emotion wash over her. She had always been self-conscious about the scar on her back, a reminder of a past injury. But to Abhiman, it was just another part of her, something that didn't diminish her beauty in any way. And with his sweet words and loving touch, she felt her insecurities melting away, replaced by a feeling of acceptance and love.

As Abhiman continued to kiss her scar, Prisha couldn't help but think about how lucky she was to have found someone like him. Someone who not only accepted her flaws, but loved her with all her imperfections. She realized that true love wasn't about finding someone perfect, but about finding someone who loved you, flaws and all.

Their passion grows with every breath. Prisha cried out as Abhiman's lips found hers again, his kiss deep and possessive. She moaned his name, her hands tangled in his hair as she surrendered completely to the pleasure.

They moved together, their bodies in perfect synchronization. The moonlight illuminated their entwined bodies, creating a magical moment that they both would never forget.

As they reached the peak of their passion, the room was filled with a sense of euphoria. The moon seemed to shine brighter, as if blessing their union.

As they lay entangled in each other's arms, the moon slowly disappeared behind the curtains, leaving them in complete darkness. But their love, ignited by the moon, would shine forever.~~~~~~~~~~~